A Ruby, a Rug and a Prince Called Doug

The King beamed.

"Son, this is the Plan. I've decided to send you to St Charming's! There, what d'you think of that!"

There was a long silence while Doug thought about it. He cleared his throat.

"St Charming's? You mean – your old school? The one for snobby princes? The one with the ghastly uniform? The one you were expelled from?"

"Well, I wouldn't say expelled exactly . . ."

"No thanks. Not jolly likely."

"No more arguments," continued the King. "You're going to St Charming's. I'll ring for Crumple and ask him to bring champagne. This is a celebration!"

KAYE UMANSKY

A RUBY, A RUG AND A PRINCE CALLED DOUG

Illustrated by Chris Fisher

Lions

An Imprint of HarperCollinsPublishers

Contents

First published in Great Britain in Lions in 1995
1 3 5 7 9 8 6 4 2
Lions is an imprint of Collins Children's Books,
a division of HarperCollins Publishers Ltd, 77-85 Fulham
Palace Road, Hammersmith, London W6 8JB

Text copyright © 1995 Kaye Umansky
Illustrations copyright © 1995 Chris Fisher

ISBN 0 00 674794 9

The author and illustrator assert the moral right to be
identified as the author and illustrator of the work.

Printed and bound in Great Britain
by HarperCollins Manufacturing Ltd, Glasgow

CHAPTER ONE
BY GEORGE,
I THINK I'VE GOT IT!

**How it all began — King Donald's awful idea —
Doug's objections are pushed aside**

It was a grey, wet Tuesday morning, and Prince
Douglas of Morania was doing what he usually
did on grey, wet Tuesdays — he was dribbling a
ball along the palace corridors: up and down
flights of draughty stone steps, around dark
corners, concentrating on fancy footwork and
muttering things to himself like "Yeah!" and
"Goal!" and "Nice one!"

Every so often, he would take a whacking great kick and send the helmet flying off a suit of armour. Occasionally he took a header at one of the portraits, regularly hitting the nose of a tight-lipped ancestor with great skill and accuracy.

It wasn't earth-shattering, but as a way of filling in a wet Tuesday morning, it wasn't bad.

Far away in the distance, through the thick stone walls, he could hear the sound of booing. It was the beetroot farmers at the castle gates, protesting again. And who could blame them? The beetroot crop had just failed for the twentieth year running. Twenty years of continuous drizzle combined with vague promises from the palace about "putting in a proper drainage system" was enough to put anyone into a revolting mood.

"Booooo!" they were chanting in an automatic dirge. "Doon wi' t'royal fambly! Coom out here, yer royal twats, an' gi' us soome moonay!"

Doug took no notice. As far as he was concerned, the sound of booing peasants was a natural phenomenon, like the wind or the sea or something. In a way, it was quite soothing. He suspected he would miss it if it ever stopped.

He rounded a corner, came to a halt and hastily picked up the ball. This particular passage contained the door to his father's study — and King Donald didn't approve of kicking balls along corridors, even on wet Tuesdays.

Holding his breath, Doug tiptoed past — but in

vain. The door burst open and the King came scuttling out, eyes rolling and hair on end, shouting, "I've got it! I've got it! By George, I think I've got it!" which was unoriginal but guaranteed to get attention.

"What?" asked Doug, with a little sigh. "What have you got, Dad?"

"What d'you think?" bellowed King Donald, clapping him painfully on the back. "The answer, of course! How to save the kingdom! At long last, everything's going to be all right. In you come, and I'll tell you all about my brilliant plan. And you can leave that ball outside. What have I told you about playing with balls indoors?"

Doug resignedly allowed himself to be frogmarched into the study. This happened every so often. King Donald had a sort of up-and-down personality. Most of the time he was up. For months at a time he could sail along quite happily, losing vast sums of money at the racetrack or over interminable games of cards with shady characters called Nobby in small, smoky back rooms. A confirmed gambler, he was always convinced that the next horse or game of snap would make his fortune. So sure was he of this that he would conveniently push to the back of his mind all the little problems that beset Morania — such as mounting debts, dwindling treasure, the lack of a decent drainage system, beetroot uprisings and so on.

But every so often, without any warning, he would have a mood change. His anxiety level would start to rise, closely followed by an attack of raging guilt, and he would set about trying to Save Morania. This was obviously one of those occasions.

"Sit down, lad, sit down, make yourself comfortable," ordered the King, pushing Doug firmly into a leather armchair.

"So what are you going to do this time?" enquired Doug, stifling a little yawn. "Get some more I LOVE MORANIA carriage stickers printed? Go on another tour of the beetroot fields and shake hands with a few peasants? Hide the cheque book from Mum?"

"Better," beamed the King. "Much, much better. Now, listen carefully, because this involves you."

Doug looked up, startled. He didn't like the sound of this. King Donald chortled and rubbed his hands, then dropped the bombshell.

"Son, this is The Plan. I've decided to send you away to St Charming's! There. What d'you think about that?"

There was a long silence while Doug thought about it.

"I said, what d'you think about that?" repeated the King. Doug cleared his throat.

"St Charming's? You mean — your old school?"

"The very one," beamed the King.

"The one for snobby princes? The one with the ghastly uniform?"

"Now, just a minute there ..."

"The one you were expelled from?"

"Well, I wouldn't say expelled exactly ..."

"No thanks. Not jolly likely."

"Oh, but Douggie, you'll love it!" cried the King, leaping to his feet and scrabbling about on his chaotic desk. "I was clearing out my desk, and I came upon this old brochure. Listen. 'Attractively set amongst delightful pine trees, St Charming's School for Young Princes and Noblemen lies in its own charming grounds on the outskirts of Nubb, City Of A Thousand Surprises, the bustling capital of Far-Off Cummerband. The well-appointed dormitories are decorated in baroque style ...'"

"Excuse me, Dad," interrupted Doug. "Why me?"

"Because you're the answer to all our problems," explained King Donald, glowing with enthusiasm. "Don't you see? You go to St Charming's and meet lots of well-connected rich boys with more gold than sense and a burning desire to invest in Moranian beetroots. Then all our troubles will be over. Play your cards right, and you might manage to marry one of their sisters, eh?"

"Dad, you're disgusting."

"No I'm not. Just think, son. You get lessons in it. Kingdom Management, I mean. You'll learn how to Rule. Firmly but wisely. Ah, me! If only I'd paid more attention when I was at school, Morania wouldn't be in the mess it is today. Chance of a lifetime, son, and I blew it."

King Donald banged his fist in theatrical despair on his desk. Piles of unpaid bills and old copies of *The Turf* slid to the floor.

"What makes you think I'll do any better?" asked Doug.

"Of course you will. You know how hopeless your mother and I are at running things. You're much cleverer. You'll come home and sort everything out and everyone'll be rich and happy."

"I wouldn't rely on it." Doug was really alarmed now. "For pity's sake, Dad! I don't want to go to some snooty boarding school. Apart from anything else, it's miles away in Far-Off Cummerband! Abroad! Away from Morania! In an entirely different country! There might be strange food and weird customs. It might not rain all the time. It's over the mountains and far away!"

"Two days' ride at the most."

"But I'll get carriage-sick!"

"Take a paper bag."

"I'll get homesick."

"We'll see you in the holidays. Oh, come on,

son. It's a wonderful school. There's simply nowhere else like it. All the best princes go there. Good old St Charming's. Best days of my life. I think."

A small shadow of doubt crossed the royal countenance, but lingered only for a moment.

"I wonder if Mr Whippy's still head," mused the King.

"Who?" asked Doug.

"Josiah T. Whiplash. The Headmaster. We called him Mr Whippy. My, what a tartar he was. Ran the school with a rod of iron. But then, your mother spoils you: you could do with a bit of discipline. I'll write you a Letter Of Introduction. You know, I simply can't think why I haven't thought of this before. It'll be the making of you. I mean, look at the state of your shirt. When was the last time you had a haircut? Kicking a ball around all day long? It's boring for you here in Morania."

"I like being bored. I'll wash my shirt. I'll get a haircut."

"But just think, son. Fabled Nubb, City Of A Thousand Surprises! The school's only a short ride away. Shops, markets, hustle and bustle. You'll love it there."

"I won't. I don't like surprises."

"Bet you anything you will. I'm sure I did."

Again, the look of doubt flickered across the King's face.

"Although, actually," he admitted, "come to think of it, I can't remember ever getting to see Nubb itself. I was always In Detention at weekends. Forced to sit in a rat-infested freezing dungeon and do long division. Ah well, no doubt I deserved it. You, you're different. You'll love it."

"No I w—"

King Donald grabbed Doug by the shoulders and shook him.

"You'll love it and that's an order! Think of it, lad. Lots of jolly chaps your own age. They've probably got new methods these days, all sorts of fancy stuff. Just imagine, son. Ballroom dancing!"

"Dad …"

"Fencing! Archery! Horsemanship! Tips on how to handle a glass slipper!"

"Dad …"

"And every other Thursday you get dumped in impenetrable forests to practise hacking your way through! That was always good for a laugh. Gosh, I haven't thought about that for years. I don't think they ever did find young Florimund …"

King Donald gave a nostalgic little chuckle.

"Dad, I …"

"Waking maidens with kisses! Now, there's a popular option. Although you don't get to do that until the third year, of course. I seem to recall I did quite well in that, ha, ha! Don't tell your mother."

"Dad, I …'

"And then, of course, there's all the jolly boy fun stuff! Pillow fights! Secret card games behind the stables! Midnight feasts in the dorm! Ducking new boys' heads down the privy!"

"Dad! Please! Will you just listen for one minute? Look, St Charming's is for rich boys. We're not rich, remember?"

"No, but we're royal," pointed out King Donald. "That still counts for something, you know."

"You'll still be expected to pay the fees. Where does the money come from?"

"Don't you worry your head about that, son. There are quite a few bits and bobs floating around in the old treasury. Sure to be some long-forgotten family heirloom we can dredge up. Mr Whippy is an antique-lover. It's his hobby. Show him a medieval toasting fork and he's anybody's."

It was getting worse and worse. Doug had one last try.

"Dad, I'll mess it up. I know I will. I won't fit in at St Charming's. They'll all be called Florizel or Ferdinand or Fritz! My name doesn't begin with an F! And I'm not wearing that idiotic uniform."

"Ah! Glad you mentioned that!"

King Donald waved a warning finger. "Now, as an old boy, Douglas, let me give you a tip. At St Charming's, they don't call it a uniform. They call it The Costume. Lots of lace and ribbons and stuff. Slashed doublet of powder-blue velvet with gold frogging, as I recall. Matching blue hose. The old school ruff, of course. And the unmistakable world famous hat trimmed with peacock feathers. And the, er — the mock sword."

"I'm not doing it," said Doug stubbornly. "I'm not wearing a cardboard sword with fake jewels on the pommel."

"Of course you will. It's traditional. You don't get a proper sword until you pass your grade three fencing exam. It's a sword to be proud of. There's a portrait of me wearing it over the fireplace in the great hall."

"I know. I've seen it," said Doug, unable to keep the horror out of his voice.

"In fact, I do believe my old Costume's still hanging up in the back of one of my wardrobes. I'll get Crumple to dig it out and give it an airing. Now, no more arguments. You're going to St Charming's, and that's final. Run along and find your mother, and I'll ring for Crumple and ask him to bring champagne. This is a celebration!"

CHAPTER TWO

DOESN'T HE LOOK SWEET?

Doug has a Costume fitting — Travel arrangements are discussed — The rug is examined — The problem of finding a suitable guard is solved

"Oh darling! Darling, you look absolutely sweet. And I love the dinky little mock sword."

Queen Deirdre had just breezed in from a shopping spree, having spent the whole morning running amok in Gowns R Us (Morania's one and only dress shop). She stood in a sea of bags and boxes, misty-eyed with admiration as Doug endured his final fitting.

Doug bit his lip and said nothing. The doublet was cutting in, the ruff was scratching his chin and the unfamiliar hose were making his legs itch. The shoes were too tight, the hat looked ridiculous — and as for the sword ...!

His beribboned reflection in the full-length mirror scowled back as Crumple, the ancient, trusted family retainer, creaked laboriously around with pins and tape measures, pulling and tugging and taking endless notes of all the alterations.

"Call me old-fashioned, but I do like the traditional Costume. It's so — royal looking. What do you think, Donald? Doesn't he look sweet?" trilled Queen Deirdre.

"Yes, yes, very nice, very nice indeed," agreed King Donald without looking up. He was sitting at the table drafting Doug's Letter Of Introduction. From the expression on his face, it was giving him trouble.

"I can't believe I'm losing my baby!" cried Queen Deirdre, reaching for a hanky and giving her eyes a theatrical little dab. "Oh, I do hope you'll be all right, darling. Which coach are you giving him, Donald?"

"The old brown one."

"And which horse?"

"The old brown one. Deirdre, I'm trying to write this letter, dearest."

"Oh, Donald! Can't he at least have the green

coach? The brown one's so tatty."

"The green one's been sold, dear, don't you remember? And before you ask, so has the green horse."

"What about the black? Oh no, he can't have that one, I need it for shopping. All right, he'll have to have the brown one. But who's going with him in the coach? To guard him, I mean?"

"Mmm. As a matter of fact, I hadn't thought of that. Can't spare any of the regulars. There's another beetroot uprising starting. Need every guard we've got."

"Can't I travel on my own?" asked Doug.

"Well, I don't see why n—" began King Donald, but he was overruled.

"Donald! Of course he must have a guard! It's expected. We don't want people thinking we can't afford one, do we?"

"Talking of money," said Doug, "what am I supposed to be paying the school fees with? Beetroots?"

"Don't be sarcastic, darling. We thought we'd give you that lovely old antique rug from the cellar. Now then, Donald, about a guard ..."

"I beg your pardon?" chipped in Doug. "Did I hear you say the old rug from the cellar? The one that used to be in the living room? The one with the tea stain in the middle? The one the cat had kittens on? With that awful pattern? The rug Dad's friend was sick on? The one all the dogs–"

"Oh, do stop fussing, darling! It's a perfectly good rug. As a matter of fact, it's an heirloom, isn't it, Donald? Have one of the servants bring in it in, Crumple. Let's have a look at it."

Crumple bowed his head in assent, climbed painfully up from his knees, carefully removed some pins from his mouth and shuffled towards the speaking tube in a corner of the room. Once there, he got his breath back and blew into it three times before issuing some muffled orders to the minions far below.

"Can I take this off now?" said Doug, not very hopefully.

"No," said Queen Deirdre. "Donald, I really would like to get this business of Douggie's bodyguard settled."

"Hmm. Well, if it's any consolation, son, I doubt very much whether you'll get attacked," said King Donald, signing the troublesome Letter Of Introduction with a triumphant flourish and placing it in a crisp white envelope, which he stamped with the royal seal. "Not by our lot, at any rate. Oh, I know they're fed up and all that, but underneath it all they're good sorts, don't you think, Deirdre? What's that you've just bought, my love? In the bags?"

"Just a couple of new gowns and a few pairs of shoes, dearest. Nothing special," said Queen Deirdre carelessly.

"I thought we were trying to save money, dear," the king reminded her.

"Were we? Oh yes, so we were. I quite forgot. Oh well, it's only gold. Douglas will sort everything out when he gets back from school. He'll be able to explain to us all about savings and things. And of course, Daddy's right, Douglas. You've nothing to fear from our lot. They're only peasants. It's not as if they've got proper weapons, is it? Only scythes and pitchforks and things."

"Oh good," said Doug heavily. "That's all right then."

"Yes, old chap, you'll be quite safe until you get past our border," continued his father. "Of course, after that, it's anybody's guess. It's years since I made the journey to Far-Off Cummerband. There's a nasty mountain pass and I seem to remember a wood ... come to think of it, there *was* a bit of bother ..."

"Which is why he's got to have a guard," interrupted Queen Deirdre firmly. "Quite apart from the look of the thing."

At this point, there came a thunderous rapping at the door.

"That will be the underling with the rug, Ma'am," intoned Crumple, shuffling over to open the door. Just before he got there, it flew open in response to a hefty kick.

"Blimey!" said a voice. "Them stairs is a bit of a wassit, ain't they? Talk about sweat."

Everyone stared curiously at the speaker, who stood in the doorway mopping his big, red face with a cloth cap. He was wearing a stained smock and big, muddy boots. His ears stuck out. There was a straw in his mouth. The rolled rug was balanced on one shoulder.

"Where d'you wannit, Missus?" he asked. Crumple frowned and tutted and waved a disapproving finger. This was no way for underlings to speak to Royalty.

"Stand up straight, fellow!" he hissed. "And kindly address Her Majesty as Ma'am." He turned to the Queen with an apologetic air. "I'm sorry, Ma'am, you just can't get the staff. Run along now, fellow, that will be all."

But the underling had just spotted Doug. His eyes lit up.

"Struth! You do look posh, guv, an' no mistake. Thas some outfit, that is. Nice stockin's."

Crumple rolled his eyes to heaven, clutched at his chest and staggered a bit.

"They're called hose," said Doug. "Not stockings. Hose."

"Get away! And would that be a mock sword you got there?"

"Yes. Isn't it sweet?" said Queen Deirdre. "Now, if you would just spread the rug out for us, my good fellow …"

"Right away, missus. Ray's the name, by the way."

22

Ray the underling heaved the rug off his shoulder and on to the floor. A huge cloud of dust rose up, setting everyone choking. When the air finally cleared, all five of them stared at the rug, now spread out in all its glory. It had probably once been a thing of beauty — but years of feet and dogs and spilled cups of tea had taken their toll. The once-proud golden dragons breathing fire in a bright blue sky had mutated into a couple of crocodiles being violently sick into a bucket. The weave was so stained and worn that there was hardly any colour left, apart from a faint hint of greyish-blue around the edges, where it met with the ragged fringe.

"I'm taking that?" said Doug.

"Well, it's past its best, I'll give you that," agreed Queen Deirdre.

"It's supposed to be past its best. It's antique," explained King Donald, sounding peevish. "Genuine antique Hartustandi, that rug. Woven by the legendary Hartustandi weavers. From the mountains of Hartustand."

"Genuine what?" asked Douglas. "Where? Who?"

"Hard ter standy," supplied Ray helpfully. "You wanna wash yer ears out, guv."

Crumple went pale and had to go and sit down in a nearby chair.

"Never heard of them," said Doug.

"You've never heard of the Weavers of

Hartustand? Good gracious me, what do they teach you in school these days?" tutted the King.

"I don't go to school," Doug reminded him.

"Well, we're about to remedy that. Yes, that rug was presented to my great-great-grandfather by the Shah of Hartustand. A gambling debt, so the legend goes. There's an ancient document — a certificate or something — that goes with it. I've got it in my desk somewhere. This rug, you may be assured, is a collector's item. Mr Whippy'll love it."

"Right," said Queen Deirdre brightly. "If it'll get Doug into St Charming's, that's all that matters. Roll it up, please, Ray. And put it on top of the brown coach. Now then, Donald. Let's get back to the question of a guard for Douglas."

"I don't want a guard," said Doug sullenly.

"Well, I'm sorry, darling, but you must. Otherwise I'll never hold my head up on parents' day. Oh Donald, surely there must be somebody who won't be missed? I mean, they wouldn't have to be experienced or anything: it's not as though they'll have to do any real fighting. They just have to wear armour and look tough."

"Armour?" breathed a voice. Everyone turned to look at Ray. He was caught in a shaft of light from the window. He had taken the straw from his mouth. His arms dangled at his sides and his fists were clenching and unclenching. His ruddy face was ecstatic and he was staring into the distance as though he could hear a choir singing.

"Did you say armour? Cor, there's a thort. I'm only a simple lackey, but iss always been my dream to wear armour an' guard somebody."

"I had a horrible feeling he was going to say that," said Doug to no one in particular.

"Really, Ray? And do you have any experience?" enquired Queen Deirdre brightly.

"Oh yeah. Me grandad was bouncer down the Snail 'n' Beetroot. 'E taught me everythin' I know."

"Of course, you'd have to be very loyal," said Queen Deirdre, staring at him.

"Catch me desertin' the guv in 'is hour o' wassit," said Ray earnestly.

"And cheap," added King Donald.

"I'll do it free," said Ray. "If only for the honour. And the armour."

"Crumple, take him to the armoury," said King Donald. "He's hired."

CHAPTER THREE
IT'S ALL IN THE JEANS

**The discontented peasants — The brown coach
and its inhabitants — Assault with a deadly
beetroot — A discussion about clothing — Ray
has lunch and a slight accident**

Three days later, a small group of discontented
peasants huddled in the drizzle by the side of a
road. Behind them, as far as the eye could see,
stretched flooded fields of submerged beetroot.

You could tell the peasants were discontented
because they were grumbling amongst themselves.
There was a lot of disgruntled head-shaking, and
quite a bit of disgusted spitting. There was even

the odd bit of fist-waving. From the general craning-of-necks and standing-on-tiptoe-whilst-restlessly-peering-down-the-road, it was evident that they were expecting something.

Whatever could it be? A delivery of mulch? The post, perhaps? Then:

"'Ere it do come," said one of them. There was a general stirring. Umbrellas were put to one side. Sleeves were rolled up, ready for business. Straws were removed from mouths. Hard, round objects were taken from pockets and hefted impatiently ...

A shabby old brown coach came lurching out of the mist, pulled by a old, brown horse. It was a scratched, faded, dirty coach with flaking paintwork and rusty lanterns. Bits creaked that shouldn't. Things ground that should have glided. Both doorhandles were missing. Quite frankly, it was the kind of coach that didn't deserve to have things thrown at it. It had been through too much already.

But try telling that to a bunch of discontented peasants.

"Right, lads, altogether now. One, two, three..."

"Boooooo!" bellowed the discontented peasants, pelting the coach with beetroots. "Doon wi' t' Moranian royal fambly! Booooooooo!"

"Take that, yer royal git!"

The coachman (an anonymous hump in a

hooded cloak) deflected the flying vegetables with his umbrella and clicked to the brown horse, who heaved a small sigh and ignored him. Nobody had bothered to give this particular horse a name, but if they had, it would most probably have been something dull, like Browny. It was the sort of horse who looked as though it had been specially bred to trudge through drizzle.

"Booo!" persisted the peasants. "Doon wi' King Donald!"

"An' that jumped up Queen Deirdre an' all!"

"An' yoong Prince Dooglas! Doon't ferget 'im! It's 'is fault too!"

One of the discontented peasants didn't go along with this. He dug the last speaker in the ribs.

"Nay, Ned, doon't be like that, yoong Doog's all reet."

"Aye, Amos, but e's still a member o' t' royal fambly, am I reet?"

"Yer reet. Booooo! Doon wi' t' lot of 'em!"

As the coach trundled by, the peasants caught a glimpse of a hat looking out at them through the spattered window. It was such a splendidly extravagant affair, this hat, that no one even noticed the glum face beneath. Then, suddenly, the window shot down and a different head stuck out. It wore a black leather balaclava, and round its neck was a studded collar.

"You geroff, you cheeky wassits!" shouted the

head. "You leave my guv alone, d'you 'ear? Show a bit o' respeck an' tug yer forelocks in a proper manner! 'Else it'll be the worse fer you!"

"Grrrr," snarled the discontented peasants, looking around for more beetroots to hurl. But there wasn't any point, for the coach had been swallowed up by the mist.

One or two of the discontented peasants lobbed another couple of beetroots anyway – more to get rid of them than anything. Then they wiped their hands, picked up their umbrellas and looked at each other.

"'Oo were that?" said Amos.

"Didn't you recognise him? That were young Ray. Raymond's lad," Ned told him.

"Were it? You mean, Ray, son of Raymond, son of Old Raymond who used to be doorman down t' Snail 'n' Beetroot? I thought 'e were workin' on a fish stall."

"'E was. Got given the push. Too cheeky to the customers. Last I 'eard 'e was workin' oop at t' palace in a servile capacity. Underling or menial or soomin'."

"Lackey, I 'eard," chipped in another peasant knowledgeably.

"An' now 'e's a bodyguard. Really comin' doon in t'world," said Amos sadly, shaking his head.

"'Ere! That were yoong Prince Doog in the coach, weren't it?" interrupted another called Seth, sounding doubtful.

"Looked like it. Did you see that 'at, though? Not 'is usual style at all. A bit oover the top, like."

"Wonder where 'e's off, then?"

"On 'oliday, by the look of all t' looggage. All reet fer some."

"Weren't that a rooll o' carpet up on't top? You doon't take carpet on 'oliday, do yer?"

"'Ow should I know? I'm a peasant. I doon't goo on 'oliday."

"Oh well," said Amos. "That's it. That's today's excitement over and done with. Might as well go 'oom. What you got foor lunch, Ruben? Noo, doon't tell me. Beetroot."

Dispiritedly, they trailed off across the fields.

"That told 'em," chuckled Ray, rummaging in his bundle for a chicken leg.

"Did you have to say that?" enquired Doug, shifting about uncomfortably on the slatted seat. The Costume was still horribly painful, despite Crumple's adjustments.

Ray paused with the chicken leg halfway to his big, red face.

"Say what?"

"The bit about tugging their forelocks. I hate it when people tug their forelocks."

Ray looked bewildered.

"Why's that then, guv?"

"Because it's class distinction. It implies that

I'm better than them in some way," explained Doug.

"Yee … aah …?" said Ray slowly, his brow furrowed in concentration, obviously waiting for more.

"Which I'm not," Doug added.

"Oh, but you are, guv, you are!" cried Ray loyally. "What, you an' them scruffy, no-account peasants? No comparison. I mean, for a start, you live in a palace wiv proper plumbin' an' that. 'N' you wear posh clothes. Suits you, you know, that there Costume. Iss not everyone kin carry off powder blue. An' all that gold pipin' stuff. Wassicalled again? Toadin'."

"Frogging," Doug told him. "It's called frogging."

"Thassa one!" cried Ray. "Froggin'! 'Course, I couldn't get away wiv it. I'm more of a levver man meself. Talkin' of which," he added shyly, "what d'you think of the outfit?"

Doug looked at him. There wasn't a square centimetre that wasn't covered with straining leather, dripping with chain mail or sprouting rivets and spikes. Ray favoured skull shaped buckles and studded wristbands. He wore a lot of thongs. Thongs were his thing.

"Very nice," said Doug.

"It is, ain't it? 'Course, the Look goes wiv the job, like," went on Ray through a mouthful of chicken. "I mean, if you're a bodyguard, you gotter look 'ard, right? Else no one'd take you serious."

"I suppose not," said Doug. "You've — er — not done much in the way of guarding before, then, Ray?"

"Nope. Never done much in the way of nothin', unless you count sellin' fish. Got the boot from that. They told me I didn't know me plaice. In fact, guv, I'll be frank with you. I ain't never amounted to much. This is an important career move for me."

Ray tore off another bit of chicken and settled back, in storytelling mode.

"I've always wanted to be a bodyguard. Or a doorman. Sorta person people look up to. Acherly" – he gave a shy little giggle – "acherly, I sometimes feels I was born for this, you know? Like it's in me oojamaflips. You know. They floats round in yer blood. Summink like trousers …"

"Genes?" guessed Doug.

"Thassem!" cried Ray happily. "Thass the little so 'n' sos. Yer, iss all in the jeans. Carnt fight yer dentistry."

"Destiny," supplied Doug automatically.

"That too. You know, guv, I like you. You're a regular bloke, you are. Fancy a suck o' me chicken leg?"

"No thanks."

"Spoonful o' me Aunty Nelly's 'ome bottled pig's foot jelly? I got plenty."

"No."

"Lump o' black puddin'?"

"No, really. I'm not hungry."

"Nervous, eh? Don't you worry, guv, you'll be all right wiv me. I'll proteck yer. I got the reflexes of a coiled zebra."

Ray gave a nod and a wink and rolled his eyes meaningfully up to the rack, where swords, knives, axes, cudgels and a large spiky thing on a chain were stacked, all ready to be seized at a split hour's notice.

"Cobra," said Doug. "It's a coiled cobra."

"Thassa one. Ooops!"

The coach gave a sudden lurch. Ray's greasy chicken bone shot from his hand and fell in Doug's lap.

"Sorry 'bout that, guv," cried Ray. "All over yer nice new stockin's too. 'Ere, I'll rub it orf ..."

"No, no, leave it!" cried Doug. He couldn't keep a certain edge from his voice. "I'll do it, I'll do it, just leave it, all right?"

"'Orl right, orl right. No need ter shout."

"And they're hose, all right? Not stockings. Hose!"

"Orl right! Just tryin' ter 'elp."

Ray sat back and watched in hurt silence while Doug dabbed at the stain.

"No need ter shout," he muttered again after a bit.

"Sorry," said Doug. "I'm a bit edgy, that's all."

"Think nuthin' of it, guv," said Ray, cheering up instantly. "Bound to be. Off to a new school an' all that. Far away from 'ome. Understandable."

Just then the coach lurched into a pothole, and Doug cracked his forehead painfully against the window. One of the feathers adorning his world-famous hat got severely bent, but Ray wisely decided not to say anything. The guv was depressed. He could see that. He needed cheering up.

"'Ere, tell yer what, guv," he cried. "Let's 'ave a game of I-spy, shall we? Make the time go quicker, eh? I got a good one, so I'll start. I Spy Wiv My Little Eye summink beginning wiv B."

"Beetroot," said Doug wearily.

"Cor. That was quick," said Ray wonderingly. "'Ow d'you get it so quick? Your turn."

Outside, the drizzle turned to proper rain. There were many, many kilometres to go. And this was only the first day.

"I don't want to play," said Doug.

CHAPTER FOUR

COME AND GET IT

**A new road and a bright morning — Ruby
Grubb waits for a lift — A horrible encounter
with a coach**

Ruby Grubb sat chewing a plait and reading
under a spreading chestnut tree by the side of a
country road. Speckled sunlight fell on her bright
red cloak. A bunch of flowers lay at her side. By
her feet was a basket covered with a checked
cloth.

Despite her relaxed air, Ruby's thumb was
ready to leap into action at the first sign of a
possible lift. Spread open on her lap was a book

entitled *One Hundred Examples Of Nasty Poisonous Toadstools*. Ruby was on number forty-seven.

"Old Man's Knees," read Ruby. "Yellow-spotted, highly poisonous, cold and slimy to the touch, good for a fever, best picked in moonlight, store in a cool place out of the reach of children."

She smiled complacently. At this very moment, in her basket, there was a perfect specimen of that very same toadstool, wrapped in cloth, along with several other interesting items.* She'd done well. Gran would be pleased.

A warm wind set the branches rustling. This was forest country, without a beetroot in sight.

On the whole, Ruby was feeling cheerful. Old Gaffer Naffleton and his chicken wagon were due round about now. If she dropped a curtsey and asked nicely, he would probably take her through Freezifoot Forest as far as the Pudding Cross turn-off. If she was lucky, he might be going as far as Nubb itself. Meanwhile, the day was still new, the sun was shining, her cloak had been cleaned, she was wearing her best button-boots, and — this was the best part — she was off to stay with Gran for a few days. At Gran's she would have her own room instead of having to share

---

Assorted herbs, two apples, a bird book, a jar of jam, a lump of cheese, a piece of elastic and a heavy sponge cake.

with Pearl, Sapphire and Coral.* At Gran's, she could stay up late and eat whatever and whenever she wanted. At Gran's, she could come and go as she pleased. No one asked her to mind the baby, or wash up. Yes, it would be nice to get away for a bit.

Her eye fell on the flowers she had picked. Old Lady's Merangue, Sissyfoot, Purple Spinaker, Fogeyberry — a charming selection, though she said it herself. There hadn't been any wolves hanging around while she picked them either, which made a pleasant change. In fact, everything was going rather well for once.

She reached under the checked cloth and took out an apple which she polished carefully on her cloak.

A small, bright-eyed bird on a nearby branch hopped closer, head on one side.

"Hello, little dicky bird," said Ruby, in the high-pitched, sugary tones that people usually reserve for talking to birds, babies and small fluffy things in general. "Who's a nice little birdy, then? Come on, come closer, don't be afraid. You're a Lesser Spotted Forkbilled Marsh Niblet, am I right?"

"Come on, then, little Marsh Niblet. Come and

---

* Three mean sisters, all older than her, who spent all day doing each other's hair and whispering about boys.

get the nice apple. Come to Ruby. Come and get it, little fellow ..."

She was wrong. The bird was, in fact, a sparrow. However, it had its eyes on the apple and wouldn't have dreamt of saying so. Ruby took a bite, spat it into her palm and held it out, making encouraging tweeting noises. The sparrow fluttered to a lower branch.

There was the sound of approaching hooves. Good old Gaffer Naffleton, dead on time as always. Ruby leapt to her feet, thumb up, sweet smile firmly fixed in place ...

And Doug's coach crashed around the corner and sprayed her from head to foot in mud.

**Ray wakes up — Some account of the journey
so far — A happy discovery**

"'Ere, what was that? Thort I 'eard far orf angry
screechin'," said Ray, juddering out of sleep with a
snort and looking about him wildly.

"You did. We nearly ran over a simple country
lass," Doug informed him dryly. He made a
mental note to have a strong word with the
coachman about reckless driving.

"No kiddin'?"

Ray sat up, adjusted his balaclava, scratched

beneath his chain mail and rubbed his eyes.

"Just dozed orf there fer a minute or two," he explained with a tinge of guilt. He had a feeling he should have been up guarding. "Where are we now then, guv?"

"Who knows?" said Doug with a tired shrug. "It's not raining and I haven't seen any beetroots, so it can't be Morania. Far-Off Cummerband, maybe?"

"Funny," said Ray. "Don't seem that far off now we're 'ere, do it?"

He peered blearily through the window, then shrank back, looking shocked.

"Cor," he said. "Look at all them trees. Give me the creeps. Sorta crowd in on you, don't they?"

Doug was inclined to agree with him. It wasn't that he had anything against trees as such, it was just the sight of so many of them all at once. This was because he was used to Morania, where skies were grey, vegetables were purple, and trees were poor, stunted things clinging together in worried little clumps.

"Bin asleep long, 'ave I?" enquired Ray casually.

"Fifteen hours," Doug informed him. "In fact, you dropped off during the third — or was it the fourth? — game of I-Spy. After you'd eaten the entire contents of both our food bundles."

Ray thought about this for a while.

"So what you're sayin' is, I bin asleep all night? An' it's now next day?" he enquired pathetically.

"Yep."

There was another pause.

"Er ... nothin' 'appened, I s'pose? Durin' the night? While I was ... er ... restin'? No emergencies?" he asked uncomfortably.

Doug thought about the night before. Any emergencies? Well ...

There was the bit with the howling hill goblins for starters. The minute they had crossed the Moranian border and begun the long climb into the mountains, the goblins had come running up from behind, waving their spears and shouting insults in some rude-sounding language. Even the horse had felt compelled to make an effort to get away from them, increasing its customary plod to a shambling trot.

Then there was the drama of the slowly-collapsing bridge across the precipice, followed by an endless wait in Little-Teetering-On-The-Edge or some such place while the coachman changed a broken wheel and the horse ate an entire window-box full of somebody's edelweiss.

The whole village had come out to stare at Doug and point at his Costume. A goat had nibbled his mock sword. Milkmaids had nudged each other and giggled behind his back. The fact that he was a Prince of the Realm hadn't cut much ice in the mountains.

Mind you, it hadn't back home either.

He had been quite relieved to get back into the

coach after that. So it was a great pity that he had had to get out again so soon after, because the horse sicked up the edelweiss and needed to lie down for a bit.

Nightfall had brought its usual problems. No pretty scenery to distract him from the horrible danger of it all. Just endless hours of jogging along precipitous tracks through the dark, stopping every so often on the edge of a ravine to allow the coachman to mutter madly over a map.

Emergencies, did he say? Yes, there had been emergencies all right.

However, things could have been worse. Ray could have woken up. And now he had, and was demanding a full account of the journey. Doug couldn't face it.

"No," he said firmly. "No emergencies. Quite uneventful, really."

"'Ere! Wassat?" cried Ray suddenly, pointing through the window.

"Sunshine," explained Doug. "Nice, isn't it?"

"No. That writin' on the tree, look. Wassit say?"

Doug looked. Sure enough, there was a chalked message scrawled across the trunk of a large oak tree. It said:

"Great! If there's one thing I could go now, iss breakfuss," enthused Ray. "Or a wedding," he added wistfully.

"I agree," decided Doug. "I think we should stop. I'll tell the coachman."

He wasn't to know it then, but this proved to be a very bad idea.

CHAPTER SIX

NICE 'ERE INNIT?

**The Happy Cockcroach — Irwin Rockmangler
— Ray examines the menu and makes
conversation at the table — A confrontation —
Money changes hands**

"Nice 'ere, innit?" said Ray, looking round with
satisfaction at the blackened rafters and filthy
floor on which roosters stalked, goats gambolled,
cockroaches capered and smelly old dogs sat and
scratched at their fleas.

In the shadows behind the counter, a pigtailed
dwarf in a filthy apron eyed them suspiciously
whilst smearing dirt on glasses with a greasy

cloth. Behind him, on a blackened range, something sizzled unpleasantly in a pan.

Doug pushed a chicken off his lap and said nothing. Through the window he could see the coachman attempting to lead the horse to the water trough. The horse didn't seem that keen. Doug guessed it had probably heard about not drinking the water in foreign parts.

"Yer. Nice," persisted Ray. "Got wassit. Character. Reminds me of the Snail 'n' Beetroot. Oi! Waiter! A bit of service over 'ere if you please!"

The dwarf shuffled over and swiped at the rough wooden table with the greasy cloth before slapping down a menu which was so covered in stains that if you soaked it in hot water, it would have made an acceptable soup.

"Cor," said Ray, poring over it admiringly. "They got everythin' 'ere, ain't they? Roachburger, Roach Nuggets, Big Roach, Roach in a Basket ..."

"Can I help you?" interrupted the dwarf, licking his pencil in a threatening sort of way. A grubby badge on his waistcoat proclaimed that Irwin Rockmangler was At Their Service.

Reluctantly, Doug ordered a cup of tea and a cheese roll.

After a good deal of deliberation, Ray decided on the Happy Cockroach Super Supreme Special, which was Roachburger 'n' Chips and a double portion of some sort of lurid green pudding amusingly called Death By Food Poisoning.

When it all arrived, he speared a large, dirty hanky on to his spiked collar by way of a bib, bit off a huge mouthful of burger and began to talk about a boil he had recently had on his neck.

It was the longest cheese roll Doug had ever eaten.

Once the Super Supreme Special had been demolished, Ray started in on his pudding and his Aunty Nelly's verrucas.

"Think I'll just stretch my legs, wash my hands, have a word with the horse, see what the coachman's up to, get a bit of fresh air, you know," began Doug, beginning to rise.

But he never finished. The door flew open and slammed back against the rough stone wall with a resounding crash.

And there she stood. The simple country girl they had nearly run over. She wore a pink dress which clashed with her ginger hair, a mud-stained red cloak which clashed with the dress and an expression which clashed with just about everything.

"Hah! So there you are!" said the girl in ringing tones, and marched purposefully towards them, scattering hens and goats to the four winds.

"Oo-er. I fink we're in trouble," hissed Ray.

"Leave this to me, Ray. Well, well, well, what a nice surprise ..." began Doug, then uttered a pained cry as she swiped him hard on his head with her basket.

"Ouch! I say, steady on!"

"See this?" screamed the sweet young country girl, bunching up a handful of the muddy cloak and waving it under Doug's nose. "Clean on today! You folk in your posh coaches make me sick! Sick, d'you hear?"

"Now, 'old on a minute ..." protested Ray, putting down his spoon and standing up. "You mustn't go round clonkin' 'Is Royal 'Ighnesss on the bonce like that ..."

"Shut up, fatty! Who asked you to speak?" spat the girl rudely. Ray looked a bit uncertain, then sat down again. Over behind the counter, Irwin Rockmangler paused in his task of spreading dirt more evenly over the counter, leant on his elbows and eavesdropped unashamedly.

"Look, I'm awfully sorry," began Doug. "It was the coachman. He won't stop for anyone."

He tried adding a sort of wry, rueful grin. It came out looking like a silly smirk.

"Running down simple woodfolk's all your sort's good for," snarled the girl contemptuously, flicking back her ginger plaits.

"I'll have a word with the coachman," promised Doug earnestly.

"I already did," said the girl. There was an ominous little smile on her lips. "Before I hit him with my basket," she added.

Doug and Ray's eyes flicked involuntarily towards the window. The horse stood by itself in the yard, flicking its tail and casting mistrustful sideways glances at the water trough. Of the coachman there was no sign.

"I, er — hope he's sorry," said Doug.

"Oh, he's sorry all right," said the girl, adding: "so are you going to pay for this cloak to be cleaned or what?"

"Yes — yes, of course I am. How much will it cost, d'you think?"

"Ten pieces of gold," said the girl immediately. "At least."

"Right. Fine."

"'Ere, 'ang on a minute, guv. Don't go givin' all yer dosh away!" wailed Ray in alarm. "That's an 'ole term's spendin' money you got there!"

"Nonsense, Ray. Where are your manners? We've ruined this maiden's cloak, and we must pay," said Doug gallantly, fishing into his doublet and bringing out a pitifully small drawstring bag.

"But she's 'avin' you on, guv ..." cried Ray. Doug ignored him.

"Will nine gold pieces be all right? With a cheque for the tenth? I'm a bit short of cash."

"I suppose so. If you've got some form of identification," said the simple country girl a little uncertainly.

"'E don't need no identification," Ray informed her. "'E's Prince Douglas of Morania and you're a cheeky girl, you are. You oughter show a bit o' respect."

"Thank you, Ray, I think I can manage this by myself, actually. Who do I make it out to?"

"Ruby Felicity Grubb. That's two Bs."

She watched silently while Doug wrote out the cheque and signed it with a flourish.

"Is that really you?" she asked disbelievingly. "Prince Douglas of Morania? Am I supposed to be impressed or something?"

"Oh, certainly not. There's nothing very impressive about being a Prince of Morania," Doug hastened to explain. "I'm terribly ordinary, really. My friends call me Doug. Do, please, think of me as a normal person."

"I think of you as a worm," Ruby told him. "And I'm surprised you've got any friends."

Doug tried his hand at a charming smile. It was similar to the rueful grin, but with more teeth.

"Here," he said. "Take the gold. And the cheque. With my compliments."

Ruby gave a sniff, took them both and slipped them into her pocket.

"Now," said Doug. "Why not let me buy you a cup of tea or something? Just to show there's no ill feeling. I think I've got a few coppers left somewhere ..."

"No ill feeling? Of course there's ill feeling.

You can keep your rotten tea. I'll take a lift, though."

"A lift? Oh, but of course! Certainly! We'll drop you off anywhere you like, won't we, Ray? Where are you going?"

"To visit my grandmother. Not that it's any of your business."

"Don't tell me, let me guess!" cried Doug. "She lives in a little cottage on the other side of the wood and is sick in bed. You're taking her some ginger wine out of the kindness of your heart."

Ruby gave him a peculiar look.

"Actually, she runs a fish stall in Nubb," she said. "And she's in the peak of health and I'm taking her a sponge cake and some herbs and stuff. And there *would* have been a bunch of flowers, except you ruined them."

"I worked on a fish stall once," Ray said to no one in particular.

"Well, come on, then. Let's go," said Ruby, and turned on her heel. Irwin Rockmangler came out from behind the counter, planted himself directly in front of Doug and stuck his left hand out. His right hand was holding a wooden club with a nail in it. It was a subtle ploy, but it worked.

"Right. Fine. Er — I'll just pay, then. You go on ahead with Ray, Miss Grubb, and get in the coach."

But she had already flounced out of the door.

CHAPTER SEVEN
AN EMERGENCY, I THINK!

The road through the Forest — Doug receives a
lecture on woodcraft — The flight — The
pursuit — Ray feels unwell — A catastrophic
accident

"What's the name of this wood?" asked Doug,
trying to keep the anxiety in his voice down to a
minimum.

"It's a forest, not a wood. We're not in it
properly yet — this is just the outskirts. And it's
name is Freezifoot," Ruby told him. "Why?"

Doug felt encouraged. It was the first time she

had spoken since setting out. Most of the time she just sat bolt upright as far away from him as possible with her basket on her lap, staring out of the window with a face like a wet Moranian Monday.* On the seat opposite, Ray was noisily sleeping off the effects of the Happy Cockroach Super Supreme Special.

"Pass the pickles, Mum," he mumbled through dreaming lips.

It wasn't a jolly party.

"So I'll know never to come here again," Doug explained. "I'm not used to all these trees at once. In Morania, there are so few trees the dogs have to queue, ha, ha."

Silence.

"That's a Moranian joke."

More silence. Then Ruby said:

"Was that gold really a whole term's pocket money?"

"Yes. Why?"

"Oh, nothing."

There was another pause. Ruby nibbled thoughtfully on a fingernail. Then:

"Actually, It won't cost ten gold pieces to have the cloak cleaned. Or anything like. I was having you on. I was mad because you ran me down. I'll give it back to you, if you like."

"That's all right. Keep it. It's only gold, as my

---

* *Or Tuesday. Or Wednesday. Or Thursday …*

parents always say. Hey, is it my imagination, or is it getting darker?"

It was. They were in the forest proper now, and the rough track had become virtually impassable. Dark trees blotted out the sun. From all sides came weird, skittering noises. Every so often, there was the flash of a yellow eye in the undergrowth, and the occasional far-off howl. Sinister branches scraped against the coachwork and threatened to decapitate the coachman (who already had a horrible headache).

"I expect you know all about forests and things," said Doug, just to keep the conversation going.

Ruby stared at him. It was a pitying sort of look.

"Oh, please don't bother to reply unless you want to," Doug told her hastily. "I'm only making idle conversation. Fellow travellers and all that."

"Of course I know about forests," said Ruby cuttingly. "I'm a woodcutter's daughter. There've been Grubbs in forests ever since the beginning of time. I know my spinneys from my thickets, I do. Stick me down in a strange wood at night with nothing but a lump of cheese and a piece of elastic and I'll find my way home by morning. Bet you couldn't do that. You or your stupid gorilla."

She glared across at Ray, who snuggled deeper into his seat, smacked his lips and said:

"Louder, Jessica, the cat's got in."

"I'm sure we couldn't," agreed Doug. "Woodcutter's daughter, eh? Fascinating."

"It is," said Ruby. "When it comes to woodcraft, we woodcutters' daughters take some beating."

"I'm sure you do," nodded Doug, his features composed into just the right expression of interested enquiry. Being a prince and having been forced into attending quite a few boring banquets in his time, it was an expression he used quite a bit.

"Do go on."

"We know all sorts of stuff. Herblore. Treecraft. Where the Horned Bogskivet lays her eggs. Where the Spongy Wart Toggart grows. How to construct a bivouac out of three sticks and an old newspaper. How to blend into the shadows."

"Well, well, well," said Doug. "Well I never did. Amazing. There's one thing I've always wanted to know about you woodcutters' daughters."

"What's that?" asked Ruby.

"If you're so good at blending in and so on, how come you always wear red cloaks? I would have thought red's the *worst* colour to wear in the woods, unless they're on fire or something. I mean, woods are mainly green, aren't they?"

Ruby gave him a look that could have stripped paint.

"That's rich, coming from someone who looks

like an explosion in a ribbon factory," she remarked coldly.

"Ah, but that's different," Doug hastened to explain. "You see, these aren't my usual clothes. You didn't honestly think I look like this out of choice, do you? This is a school uniform. I'm on my way to St Ch— Hello, what's happening?"

Suddenly, the trees no longer hugged the road and the coach began to pick up speed. In seconds, the horse's predictable plod had accelerated into an agitated canter, which in turn became a full-blown, panicky gallop.

Ruby, Doug, Ray and assorted bits of luggage and weapons were thrown violently to and fro as the coach rocked dangerously from side to side. From out front, there came the desperate crack of the coachman's whip.

There was another, more ominous crack, which came from behind.

"Wassat? Wasappnin'? Is it mornin', Mum?" wailed Ray, waking up on Ruby's lap with a start.

"Ahhh!" screamed Ruby. "Get him off me!"

"An emergency, I think! Do your stuff, Ray!" shouted Doug, ducking as Ray's knife collection rained down from the roof rack and stuck, quivering, in the floor.

But Ray's zebra reflexes refused to cooperate. He went very pale and clung tightly to Ruby. He pretended later that it was the pudding at the Happy Cockroach, but everyone knew better.

So Doug looked. He stuck his head out of the window, and risked a quick glance.

Behind — only a short way behind, and getting closer — was a masked rider. He wore a coat of claret velvet and a bunch of lace at his chin. He also sported a cocked hat, tight breeches and long leather riding boots. In his hand was a smoking pistol.

"What is it? What's going on?" yelled Ruby, trying to prise Ray's arms from around her neck.

"A highwayman!" shouted Doug over his shoulder.

"What's he look like?" Ruby wanted to know. "What's he wearing? Has he got a horrible little moustache by any chance? Ahhhh — help!"

Without warning, the forest road veered sharply to the right. The horse swerved and reared, then took off at right angles down the steep bank. The coach teetered at the edge for one heart-stopping moment. The coachman wisely took the opportunity to jump for it. He landed on his feet and scuttled off into the bushes, never to be seen again. (In this story, anyway.)

Behind him, the coach finished teetering and plunged. The traces snapped, and coach and horse parted company. The horse veered off to the left. Out of control, the runaway coach crashed straight on through trees and bushes, hit a stone, ran on two wheels for a few seconds, and then slowly keeled over.

Doug suddenly, confusingly, found himself upside down with a heavily bejewelled mock sword pommel up his nose and most of Ray on top of him. His cheek was pressed hard against what felt like a chicken leg — or it could have been Ruby's elbow. Something lumpy was sticking into his back. His hat was over his eyes. There were crashings and tinkling noises as the whole mess settled down. From outside came the sound of a slowly spinning wheel. It was all most unpleasant.

However, it wasn't as unpleasant as what happened next.

"Yeur monay or yeur life," demanded a voice.

Now, that *was* unpleasant.

CHAPTER EIGHT

ALORS, WHERE 'AVE YEU BEEN?

Our heroes are trussed and bound — Insults fly — Ray attempts diplomacy and fails — A private note is read aloud — All three are robbed and left to the mercy of squirrels

"You won't get away with this, you know!" cried Doug. It was corny, but the best he could do. Vainly he strained at the ropes which bound him to a tree. A short way away, the highwayman was busily rummaging through his trunk. Nightshirts, spare hose and other items of a highly personal nature were littered all over the glade.

"Hear hear!" agreed Ruby stoutly. "Unhand us, you great bully. Untree us, I mean."

"Sssh," muttered Ray, not at all keen to stir things up. "Don't annoy 'im."

Things had gone very badly for them over the past few minutes. Since crawling from the wreckage, they had found themselves being ordered about at pistol point, tied to trees and unceremoniously robbed of anything that took the highwayman's fancy. Ray had lost his spiky collar and skull-belt. Ruby had been politely divested of her bag of gold and Doug's cheque. Doug had also come off badly, losing both his cheque book and the traditional silver buckles on shoes. To his disappointment, the highwayman had shown no interest in the mock sword.

The horse had wandered back, and was standing around uncertainly, pretending to nibble grass. If it wasn't a horse, you would have said it looked sheepish.

"Did you hear me?" squawked Doug as a hot-water bottle sailed over the highwayman's shoulder. "I said, you won't get away with this!"

"Neu?" sneered the highwayman. "Oo says so?"

"Prince Douglas of Morania says so," Doug told him with a certain amount of pride.

"Nevaire 'eard of eem."

"Well, that just goes to show how ignorant you are!" Ruby chimed in unexpectedly. "He's got a cheque book with his name on it."

"Sssh," begged Ray in an undertone. "Don't upset 'im."

"And you can belt up, too!" snapped Doug. "Some bodyguard *you've* turned out to be!"

"Well, well, look at zis!" cried the highwayman, coming across Doug's sponge bag. "A pretty peenk toosbrush wiz ze royal crest! Zis is what I do wiz yeur toosbrush."

And he snapped it in half and threw both bits into the brambles.

"What a cheek," Ruby hissed. "Interfering with someone's toothbrush. That's really personal."

"Swine!" ground out Doug. "Cowardly knave! Show off!"

"Scuse me, sir, I fink as 'ow the guv don't really mean that," broke in Ray. "'E's 'ad an 'ard day, what wiv one fing an' anuvver ..."

"Silence, yeu!" rapped the highwayman, straightening and cocking his pistol.

"Right away, sir, no problem, 'ave a nice day," purred Ray. If the ropes had permitted, he would have tugged his forelock.

The highwayman strutted up to Doug and pushed his face unpleasantly close. He had a lot of big yellow teeth and one of those horrible, thin little moustaches which look like two tadpoles colliding head-on.

"OK, *Preence* Douglas of Morania. I 'ad enough. Stop beating ze bush around. I want ze monay. Ze real monay, not ze cheques or ze small change. Tell me where eet ees or eet weel be ze worse for yeu. Yeu seenk zis ees ze only 'old-up I got planned for teuday?"

"How many more times must I tell you? There *is* no money. I'm royalty. We don't carry money. You're wasting your time, cloth-ears."

The highwayman scowled.

"Oo yeu call zis closs-ears? Deun't yeu know oo I am?"

"I do," said Ruby with a sniff. "Worse luck."

"You do?" said Doug, startled. "I don't. Should I?"

"Hah!"

The highwayman slapped his thigh and flicked his hair back.

"My cart," he said, taking a dog-eared rectangle from his pocket with a flourish and holding it in front of Doug's nose.

Doug looked at it. It was written in bold black twirly writing and it said:

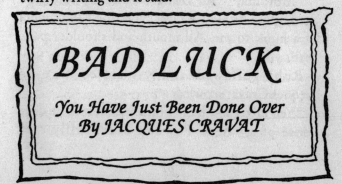

BAD LUCK

You Have Just Been Done Over
By JACQUES CRAVAT

alias

THE SINGING HIGHWAYMAN
(Signed Wanted posters available, three
guineas each, apply Bette Buxom,
The Laughing Footpad,
Lightfinger Street, Nubb)

"Who?" said Doug.

Apparently, this wasn't the correct response at all. The highwayman looked bewildered.

"Jacques Cravat," he explained. "Yeu know. Ze Singing 'Ighwayman. C'est moi. Zat ees me."

"Sorry," said Doug with a shrug.

"But I am legend in zees parts! I am, 'ow you say, 'ouse'old name. All ze maidens swoon ovaire me. Zey sink I am 'eunky."

"Not all of them," Ruby corrected him. "Only some. Only the stupid ones. Like my sisters."

"All of zem! Zey all put my Wanted postaires on zere bedroom walls! Alors, where 'ave yeu been?"

"Morania," said Doug. "I already told you. And, quite frankly, Cravat, you don't look much of a hunk to me. All mouth and shoulder pads, that's you."

Ruby guffawed, and Ray closed his eyes. Jacques Cravat scowled.

"Yeu talk a lot, huh? For someone wiz ze dress sense of a whelk. Powdair blue! Frilly ruff!

Stupeed 'at! Stockeengs! And as for zat toy sword! Pah!"

"They're called hose," Doug informed him tightly.

There was a brief silence while they curled lips at each other.

Then, Jacques Cravat snatched back his card, turned on his heel and stalked back to Doug's trunk. He scrabbled around in the bottom and came up with a slipper. He held it up for all to see then hurled it high into a tree, a malicious little smile on his lips.

"Vin wassit, ain't 'e?" whispered Ray with a shiver, watching Jacques Cravat blow his nose on a carefully folded frilly shirt before grinding it into the mud with his boot.

"Dictive," supplied Doug automatically.

"Thassa one," muttered Ray and subsided into silence.

The trunk was nearly empty. Now then. The thing was, would the highwayman discover the false bottom? Doug swallowed nervously.

"Ees empty," announced Jacques Cravat, bundling up the last pair of Doug's winter combinations and hurling them into a thorn bush. "No monay 'ere."

Douglas breathed a sigh of relief.

"Now for ze false bottom," added the highwayman with a malicious little smirk. "What yeu sink? I born yesterday?"

There was a flicker of steel, and suddenly a small knife was in his hand. It was obviously something he had practised. With a leer, he bent over the trunk. When he straightened up, there was a triumphant grin on his face. In his hand was a white envelope stamped with the Moranian royal seal (a beetroot rampant with two crossed pitchforks). The letter bore the address:

Josiah T. Whiplash (Headmaster)
St Charming's School For Young Princes
Nubb

"'Allo, 'allo, what 'ave we 'ere, I wondaire?"

"It's nothing. Just a private note from my father to the headmaster of my new school. Nothing of interest to you."

"So yeu say. Let us take a leetle look, oui?"

Sick at heart, Doug watched as Jacques Cravat ripped open the envelope and took out two pieces of paper. One was yellow and ancient looking. The second was covered with his father's writing.

Dear Headmaster, (read Jacques Cravat)
I wonder if you will remember me. Donald III, King of Morania. I am an-ex pupil of yours. Your affectionate name for me was Thickhead. I was the one who started the gambling den in the gym that time, remember?

I confess I wasn't one of your better pupils. I hope you will have more success with my son, Douglas, the bearer of this letter. He is a good chap and very willing to learn. Just as well, as his mother and I are rather relying on him to save the country from ruin.

Sadly, it has been yet another poor year for beetroot, which you may remember is Morania's chief crop. Deirdre and I sometimes wonder if it has anything to do with the weather. It does tend to rain a lot. Anyway, as a result I'm afraid we are having the usual cash-flow problems and the old coffers are currently rather low. Instead, I have sent you a very valuable rug which has been in the family for generations. It was presented to my great-great-grandfather by none other than the Shah of Hartustand.

Hartustand, you may recall, is a region renowned for the quality of its carpets. The enclosed ancient document certifies that, whilst this carpet might look like something you would use to line a kennel, it is in fact a genuine, antique, hand-crafted Hartustandi rug. I hope you like it, and trust it will cover my son's fees.

Pip pip.

H. M. Donald III

"Aha!"

Grinning broadly, Jacques Cravat tore King Donald's Letter Of Introduction into tiny pieces and sprinkled them over the muddy ground. He then refolded the certificate and carefully placed it in his breast pocket.

"Aha! Now I see! You were right — zere is no monay. Instead, zere is valuable antique rug. Now, where ees zis rug? Could zat be eet, I wondaire? Zat roll ovaire zere, strapped to ze roof of ze coach?"

"Leave that rug alone!" rapped Doug, struggling pointlessly against his bonds. "That's property of the crown, that is. Take it at your peril!"

"OK. I weel," said Jacques Cravat, striding over to the rolled rug.

And he did.

CHAPTER NINE
WOLVES AND STUFF

Ruby's ingenuity — An amazing escape — Ray is fired — Ruby proves to be a mine of information

"Oi! Stop, thief! Come back 'ere an' fight, you miserable coward!" bellowed Ray, just as soon as the galloping hooves had faded into the distance and the highwayman was safely out of earshot.

Doug and Ruby slowly turned their heads and stared hard at him.

"Juss you wait!" continued Ray, with just a shade less certainty. "Pickin' on my guv like that! I'll get you all right, juss see if I don't ..."

His voice tailed away and he swallowed. Then he tried a different tack.

"Tell you what, guv, if I 'adn't eaten that puddin' and was feelin' a bit more meself, like, I'd 'ave taken that pistol orfuv 'im an' whacked 'im into nex week, I would. I'd 'ave ..."

"Ray," said Doug. "Shut up."

"No, but seriously, guv, if I 'adn't 'ad this very narsty touch o' windy gestion ..."

"You heard. One more word and you're fired."

"But ..."

"That's it. You're fired."

Ray subsided into hurt silence. At least, there would have been silence if it wasn't for Ruby, who suddenly began to twist and turn and make the sort of grunting noises that usually indicate extreme exertion.

"Ruby?" said Doug. "What are you doing?"

"Cutting myself loose of course," said Ruby, squirming away.

"Oh yeah. With what?"

"With these scissors which I always keep secreted up my sleeve just in case something like this should ever happen," explained Ruby smugly.

"Really?" exclaimed Doug, terribly impressed. "Gosh."

"I told you we woodcutters' daughters are known for being resourceful," said Ruby airily. She gave one more wriggle, and the ropes dropped away. Rubbing her wrists, she strode over to the crashed coach, dropped to her knees and vanished from sight. When she re-emerged she was holding her basket.

"It's all right," she pronounced. "Nothing's spoilt. I tucked it out of sight beneath the seat. Lucky he didn't look."

"Oh, that's all right then," said Doug. "So glad your basket's undamaged. Any chance of cutting me loose before nightfall, d'you think? Only when you're ready, of course."

"All right, all right, no need to be sarcastic. If anyone's in a hurry, it should be me. After all, he only took your old rug. He's got my gold pieces. And the cheque! That's the first cheque anyone's ever given me."

"Old rug? *Old rug?* That was genuine Hartustandi! It was an heirloom! That *old rug*, as you put it, is supposed to pay my school fees."

"I know, I know, don't get so het up. I heard what the letter said."

She took her small scissors and began to hack through the ropes binding Doug.

"I just can't believe my rotten luck," she muttered as she worked. "Mown down, insulted, trussed up and robbed all in one morning. And it's all your fault."

"Eh? That's a bit strong …"objected Doug.

"Well, it is. You don't think he'd have bothered with me if I wasn't with you, do you? Of course it's your fault. I've a good mind not to bother with you any more. Stand still, will you. On the other hand, I can't bear to let him get away with it. He's such a show-off."

"You seem to know a lot about him."

"Oh, he's quite a local celebrity. Villages get him to come along to open up fêtes and stuff. He sometimes turns up on karaoke evenings in local inns. Fancies himself as a singer."

"But that's disgusting!" said Doug, who was tone-deaf. "He's a robber! He *robs* people. He should be put behind bars."

"Well, to be fair, he usually only robs rich people and there aren't a lot of those around here. My sisters think he's romantic. I don't. I think he's flash. Pearl's got his autograph, and Coral and Sapphire have collected all his Wanted Dead Or Alive posters. They've got the whole set. Back, front, side view, and the fuzzy one of him on his horse. Push outwards with your hands a bit ... hold still, don't be a cissy ... last bit ... there, that's got it."

Doug thankfully took a few staggery steps away from the tree and stretched his arms. Ray stared, pathetically envious.

"Right," said Ruby. "The first thing we have to do is get out of the forest. It wouldn't do to be still here at nightfall."

"Oh? And why is that?" enquired Doug, not really wanting to know.

"Oh, you know. Wolves and stuff. You go and

salvage anything that might be useful from the coach. I'll see to the horse."

"What about me?" mumbled Ray, sounding pathetic.

"What about you?" said Doug and Ruby together.

"Ah, come on, guv. You're not gonna leave me 'ere, are yer? Wiv all these trees? An' the wolves an' stuff?" begged Ray, looking quite pale.

"We might," said Doug.

"You're 'avin' me on," said Ray hopefully. There was a long pause. "Aincha?"

"Oh, come on then," said Doug with a sigh. "Pass the scissors, Ruby."

"Do I have to?"

"I won't forget this, guv," promised Ray. "You're a good mate, you are. You can rely on me. I won't let yer down again. From now on I'm gonna do what's wassit."

"Right?" guessed Doug.

"Right," agreed Ray.

CHAPTER TEN
SHOW 'IM IN, THEN, TERRY

Bette Buxom relaxes in her boudoir — A brief conversation on the subject of sausage rolls — An unexpected visitor — Jacques suffers a terrible disappointment

Bette Buxom, triple-chinned proprietress of The Laughing Footpad, known friend of thieves and highwaymen and notorious receiver of stolen goods, was reclining on her sofa in what she always referred to as her Boo Doyer.*

---

* *Boudoir. It's French.*

She wore a dress of red satin, and there were matching ribbons in her hair. Her beefy arms jangled with bracelets, and diamonds glittered at her ears and throat.

She was eating chocolates and occasionally feeding them to a number of small, shivery dogs with long fringes who snuggled on her ample red lap, staring up in bulgy-eyed adoration. Next to the sofa was a cluttered table containing dozens of back issues of *What Jewel?**; a tall thin glass of something green and sticky; half a chocolate doughnut; a jeweller's eyeglass and an open drawstring bag spilling out ropes of pearls, rings, bracelets, tiaras and an exceedingly vulgar brooch with the word SWAG picked out in opals.

There came the unmistakable sound of hooves clattering down the passage, followed by a knock at the door. The small dogs set up a chorus of shrill yapping as the bar centaur stuck his harrassed head around.

The bar centaur was a thick-set, hairy-armed chap named Terry down to the waist, at which point he became a horse called Merrylegs. As always, he was rushed off his fetlocks.

"Bette! Rats 'ave been at the sausage rolls again."

---

* *A monthly must for all discerning catburglars, fences and Queen Deirdre.*

73

"Well, you know what I told you, Terry. Stick 'em behind the pork pies. No one'll notice."

"Right you are. And you got a surprise visitor."

"I have? Male or female?"

"Male."

"Ooh, how exciting. Well, show him in, then, Terry."

The hooves clopped off down the passage. Bette patted her hair, popped a coffee cream into her mouth and chewed happily. She was feeling cheerful this evening. According to the *Nubb Gazette*, burglaries were up, and that was always a good sign. Business was brisk in the bar and there hadn't been a Troll raid in ages. Soon she could cut down on bed and breakfast and concentrate just on running the tavern and receiving stolen goods, both of which she could do lying down. All she' needed was one more major bit of business to get that extra lump sum in the bank, and that would be it — she could become a lady of leisure.

"Bette! Ma cherie!"

The door crashed open. Posing on the threshold with arms oustretched, legs akimbo and tadpoles wiggling, stood Jacques Cravat. All windblown curls and thigh boots and cocky grin and ruffled lace. Smelling strongly of cologne, triumph and horse. Over his shoulder was slung what appeared to be a rolled-up rug.

"Jacques, you naughty boy! Long time no see!

Where you been?" cried Bette delightedly. "Come over 'ere, you wicked rascal, and let me see you!"

The highwayman glanced up, hoping for a handy chandelier on which to swing across. But he had to make do with manly striding.

Bette extended a plump, beringed hand and Jacques Cravat bent and kissed it with a resounding smack. The smallest fluffy dog growled and showed its frenzied teeth. Bette simpered and coyly patted the place next to her on the sofa. Jacques reached out to clear himself a space and the smallest fluffy dog tried to bite him.

"Well?" asked Bette. "What's my favourite felon been doin' all this time, eh? Keepin' busy, I 'ope? Got summink good for old Bette? Any pretty little baubles you want me to find a good 'ome for? Knock it off, Pootsie, it's Jacques."

"'Ave I got sumpsing good?" crowed Jacques Cravat, shaking his curls and slapping his thigh. "'Ave I got sumpsing good, she ask? Oui, cherie, I 'ave sumpsing zat weel warm ze ceuckles of yeur 'eart. At last, ze Singing 'Ighwayman 'its ze jackpot! Cleuse yeur eyes."

"What you done, you scamp, gawn an' nicked the crown jewels?" asked Bette, closing her eyes with a girlish giggle.

"Bettaire," smirked Jacques, shaking out the rug.

"Well, come on then," cried Bette, quivering with greedy anticipation. "Don't keep it to yerself. Can I look yet?"

"Voilà! Now yeu can open them up. Getta loada zat!"

Bette looked down at where he was pointing. At her feet, over her nice, tasteful, scarlet shagpile, lay a hideously dirty old rug.

"Blimey!" said Bette. "Where'd you get that?"

"Yeu see? I told yeu!" crowed Jacques Cravat. "Now zen, 'ow much yeu pay me, huh, cherie? I seenk ees worth a lot of monay, huh? Genuine 'Artustandi, zis rug."

"Hmm. What are those? Look like two crocodiles bein' sick in a bucket?"

"Oo cares what zey are? Deed you not 'ear me? Zis rug ees genuine 'Artustandi."

"Hard to whatee?"

"Yeu know. 'Artustandi. Woven by ze famous Weavers of 'Artustand. Look, I show yeu. Voilà. Ze certificate."

Carefully, Jacques handed her a yellowed, folded piece of paper. Bette took it and examined it with her eyeglass.

"Found eet in ze woods," chortled Jacques, looking over her shoulder, putting a finger one side of his nose and giving a pantomime wink. "Some luck, eh?"

"What, in a ditch or somethin'?" asked Bette.

"In a ... oh, I see. You make ze fun. Ha, ha, ha.

Ees vairy good joke. Now you give me lot of monay, huh?"

"Hartustandi, eh?" said Bette, putting away her eyeglass. "Jacques, me darlin', I think you'd better sit downi. This rug ain't worth nuthin'. It's a loada rubbish. I ain't never 'eard of nowhere called Hartustand fer a kick orf. An' even if there was, so what? I mean, look at it. 'Oos gonna want that in their livin' room, eh? I mean, look at them stains."

The tadpoles on Jacques Cravat's upper lip twisted and writhed in a dance of shocked disbelief.

"But ees antique! I steal eet wiz my own 'ands! Eet belong to a *preence*! What about ze ancient document?"

"It wouldn't make no difference if it belonged to the man in the moon. Try the Saturday mornin' market in downtown Nubb. Tacky ole mats like this is ten a penny. All with forged certificates. All from places nobody's ever 'eard of. All supposed to be the rightful property of some made-up emperor or other. It's a racket, Jacques. I got discerning customers. I can't sell 'em rubbish. They trust me."

"Yeu are telling me zis rug ees worth nusseeng?"

"'Fraid not. In fact, I'd say it's a bit of a 'ealth 'azard."

"Bozzair!!"

Jacques Cravat leapt to his feet, scattering cushions and dogs with gay abandon. He stamped his boot and thrust out his lower lip.

"Now what I am supposed teu deu?" he cried petulantly.

"Leave it 'ere, pet. I'll get one of the lads to throw it out later. I'll chuck this into the bin, shall I?"

She balled up the certificate, and threw it casually into a nearby wastebasket.

"No point keeping it. Don't take on so. Some yer wins, some yer loses, right? Now, you toddle on out to the bar and ask Terry to get you a bite to eat. On the 'ouse. I can recommend the sausage rolls."

"I not 'ungry," sulked Jacques Cravat.

"Oh, come on now, all ain't lost. It's Talent Night tonight. You come on just the right evening. You can give us a bit of a song, right? Might win a prize, eh? What about a little smile for Bette. Eh? Eh? That's better. That's my boy. Now then, off you go. I'll be out to join you in a minute, just want to fix me face."

The second the door shut behind him, Bette ran to lock it, then hurried to the bin, fished out the crumpled certificate and smoothed it out reverently on her bureau.

She then hastened to the shelves that housed her impressive collection of books on antiques. She ran her eyes along the titles, pulled one down, and began to rifle eagerly through the pages.

And when she found what she was looking for, she smiled.

CHAPTER ELEVEN

PLAN? WHAT PLAN??

An unnerving walk in the forest — Two
minutes' rest — A Moranian joke —
The beginnings of a Plan — Gaffer Naffleton
finally turns up .

"Ruby? Wait a minute, can't you? My doublet's
caught up on a thorn bush! Ah, that's got it!"

"Sssssh! Whatever is the matter with you?"
hissed Ruby over her shoulder. "You're making
enough noise to waken every wolf within a ten
mile radius."

"I'd like to see you try moving quietly in these
shoes," grumbled Doug.

"Well, you shouldn't have worn them in the first place."

"You don't think I wanted to wear shoes like these do you? I keep telling you, they're part of the St Charming's Costume."

"Well, they're ridiculous. And can't you at least throw away that stupid mock sword?"

"Don't you think I've tried? I can't. It's glued on to the doublet. Ah, botheration!"

"Now what?"

"Another ladder in my hose. And stop smirking, will you? It's not funny."

They were plodding along the track in convoy. Here, the forest was particularly dense. The black trees pressed in, their tops converging overhead. It was horribly dark and from all sides came worrying, wild noises: little scuffles and low cries and patterings and the occasional manic titter. Most offputting.

Ruby strode along in front, leading the horse. She was holding aloft the one remaining coach lantern which still worked. The dim glow somehow only served to make everything seem even darker.

After her stumbled Doug in his unsuitable Costume. He was carrying a small bag containing some useful overnight things, such as half a toothbrush, a torn nightshirt and a folding mother- of-pearl shoe horn.

Last in line, after a longish gap, came Ray, with

blisters. He limped along with his thongs trailing, morosely swinging a spiked ball on a chain, which was all that was left of his impressive armoury.

"Guv? I wanna stop and 'ave a rest," bleated Ray. "Me feet 'urt."

"I thought you were supposed to be hard," Doug reminded him with a sneer.

"I am," said Ray. "Except for me feet."

"Did the gorilla speak? Does it want a banana or something?" Ruby wanted to know.

"He says his feet hurt. He wants a rest. So do I, actually. I've been through a lot today, and I'm not afraid to admit that I feel very shaken. It's not like this back in Morania, I can tell you."

"Too bad. We've got to keep moving," ordered Ruby. "Funny things can happen on this road," she added darkly.

Ray muttered something, shuffled his soft feet and looked sullen.

"What did it say?" asked Ruby, who had sharp ears.

"He wants to know how come you've got the lantern," obliged Doug. "He says he's a guard and you're just a girl. He says he's got a spiked wossit on a chain and all you've got is a basket. He thinks he ought to be the leader."

Ruby stopped.

"Look, let's get this straight," she said fiercely. "In the forest, I'm the leader. What I say goes, right? I've got the lantern because I'm so much better than you two at spotting hazards like potholes and roots and low-lying branches. Also, I'm the only one who can find the way out. Remember what I said about finding my way out of forests?"

"Something about cheese and elastic, wasn't it?" said Doug.

"That's right. Woodcraft skills. Something you know nothing about. And I might remind you that if it wasn't for me you'd both be tied to trees. If I'd had my way, *he'd* still be tied up now."

Ray opened his mouth to say something, then wisely shut it again.

"You're holding me up, you know," snapped Ruby. "I'd have been at my gran's by now if it wasn't for you lot. A bit of gratitude wouldn't come amiss."

"Sorry," said Doug humbly. "I'm sure we're very grateful. Now, could we have a rest? Please? I can't get used to walking bent double. In Morania we walk tall. Well, we do when there isn't an uprising going on. Then we duck quite a bit."

"Two minutes' rest," ordered Ruby. "Then we go on."

Doug and Ray both sank to the grass verge with sighs of relief and examined their feet. Ruby reached into her basket and brought out an apple which she waved around just long enough to get everyone's juices flowing before eating it herself.

"So what it's like in Morania?" she asked, through a mouthful of juice. "Not that I'm particularly interested."

"Wet," Doug told her. "There's more rain 'ere than anywhere. Morania. Get it? That's a Moranian joke."

"It's awful."

"Ah. Well, you see, Moranians are not noted for having a dry sense of humour," explained Doug.

Ray laughed uproariously in the hopes of getting back in the guv's good books.

"Oh, very good, Guv, very good. A dry sense of 'umour. Thassa good one, that is."

Finding himself ignored, he wandered off to sulk and to soak his feet in a nearby stream.

Ruby sat down on a log and drummed her heels.

"What'll your parents do when they find out the rug's been stolen?" she asked.

"I dread to think," said Doug gloomily. "Jump off the battlements, I should think."

"In that case we'd better make sure you get it back," said Ruby.

"Some hopes. Cravat'll be miles away by now. Arrgh! What was that?"

"Nothing. A bird. Gosh, you're very nervous, aren't you? I thought princes were supposed to be bold and fearless."

"It's all these trees," explained Doug, glancing

anxiously into the shadows. "Goodness knows what's scuttling around in them. I feel as though I'm being watched all the time."

"Oh, you are," said Ruby carelessly, holding her apple core out to the horse, who accepted it with enthusiasm. "There are always things watching. Killer squirrels. Lost babes. Wicked old witches. Crazed hermits. Wolves, of course. It's just a question of knowing which ones matter and which ones don't. That's where woodcraft comes in. You're lucky you've got me to help you."

"I know," said Doug. "Thanks. Really. We'd be in a bit of a pickle without you."

"You're in a bit of a pickle with me," said Ruby tartly. "I don't have all the answers, you know." But she sounded pleased.

"What I can't understand is why nothing's come along," she continued. "Not even a cart or anything. Normally there's quite a bit of traffic through the forest at night. I can't understand what's happened to Gaffer Naffleton. He's hours overdue. It's like some mysterious force is at work.* Oh well, not to worry. D'you want a piece of my sister's awful sponge cake? I'm taking it to Granny. It's traditional. I've got some in my basket."

---

* She was right. It was the same mysterious force that applies anywhere in the known universe when you're waiting for a bus.

"Er — no thanks," said Doug. All this talk of crazed hermits and mysterious forces was doing terrible things to his appetite. "How much further till we're out of the woods?"

"Not far. Three kilometres, perhaps. Once we're on open road we're bound to get a lift. It won't take long to get to Nubb. So we ought to discuss the plan now."

"Plan?" said Doug, taken unawares. "What plan?"

"The plan to get your rug back, of course. We've got to have a plan," said Ruby impatiently.

"We? You mean, you're going to help?"

"I think I'd better, don't you? So far, you haven't managed very well on your own."

"You're right. I'm useless," confessed Doug. "I can't even remember the name and address on the card Cravat showed me. Now, who was it again?" He clutched at his head. "Bess Bulky? Beth Beefy …?"

"Bette Buxom, The Laughing Footpad, Lightfinger Street, Nubb," said Ruby promptly.

"You know it?" gasped Doug.

"'Course I do. It's where you send for the posters. Anyway, it's where Cravat always stays when he's in Nubb. Notorious place for thieves and criminals. And they have a Talent Night which he always goes in for. Bette Buxom's the owner. She's a fence."

"Sorry?" asked Doug, startled. The only fence

he knew of was the high, purple-splattered one running around the palace which was supposed to keep beetroot-hurling peasants at bay.

"A fence. You know. A receiver of stolen goods."

"Oh, really? We don't have burglary in Morania. Nothing worth stealing, apart from umbrellas. So how do you know so much about this Buxom woman?"

"She buys her fish from my gran's stall."

"Really? Oh, but this is wonderful! Why didn't you say?"

"You didn't ask," said Ruby with a shrug.

"Can I have a piece of sponge?" asked Ray, wandering back from his stream.

Sadly, his humble little request clashed with a much more interesting and arresting noise altogether.

It was the sound of wheels.

"Gaffer Naffleton!" whooped Ruby, jumping to her feet. "Great! We can get a lift in the chicken wagon."

"How do you know?" hissed Doug. "How do you know it's not somebody else out to rob us? You said yourself there were witches and stuff ..."

But it wasn't witches and stuff. It was Gaffer Naffleton.

There was something very irritating about the way she was always right.

CHAPTER TWELVE
PLEASE PASS, RUN OUT
OF HORSE

**The entry into Nubb — Doug is impressed —
Gaffer Naffleton — An encounter with the Law
— A hurried parting of the ways**

In Nubb, it was market day. Being the capital city of Far-Off Cummerband, the place was always bursting at the seams, but on market day it really popped its buttons.

"Wow!" breathed Doug, a native Moranian whose idea of a large town was anywhere with a shop. "This is absolutely amazing! I'm impressed!"

He was clinging to the very edge of the driver's seat, next to Ruby, who was squashed next to Gaffer Naffleton. Gaffer Naffleton had predictably turned out to be a deaf, pipe-smoking rustic in a smock and floppy hat who said nothing apart from "Ar" and "Nay" and stared vacantly into the distance. No surprises there.

Ray had been consigned to the wagon with the chickens. It was either that or run behind, as there was no more room on the driver's seat.

"It's amazing! Isn't it amazing?" Doug shouted across excitedly to Gaffer Naffleton.

"Ar," said Gaffer Naffleton, sucking on his pipe.

The two donkeys pulling the wagon inched their way forward through the packed streets. Behind the wagon plodded the brown horse, looking rather put out, as any horse would who had been demoted from pulling a royal coach to bringing up the rear of a chicken wagon. Besides, it had a sore foot.

It was all too much for Doug to take in. The clutter of stalls, the shrieking traders, the women with baskets of strange fruits on their heads, the grubby urchins and mangy dogs, the unmistakable witches and wizards mingling freely with the crowds, the unbelievable assortment of coaches, carts, rickshaws, donkeys and broomsticks jostling for space on the cobblestones, the tall buildings with lines of washing flapping on every balcony — it made his head spin.

One look at Doug's open mouth and bedazzled face was all it took for a whole tribe of pedlars, beggars, sharp-eyed blind men and general riffraff to descend upon the wagon like a pack of starving wolves on a bowl of Winalot.

"Oh dear, here we go," said Ruby with a sigh. "They know you're from out of town. You might as well have a flashing sign on your head saying STOP ME AND TRY IT ON. Ignore them. Whatever happens, don't buy anything."

"Looking for somewhere to stay, my beribboned friend?" asked a foxy-faced goblin in a slouch hat, smiling a smile that would stop a chicken dead in its tracks a hundred metres away. "I know a place, The Three Jolly Conmen down by the docks, nice an' clean, very cheap, proprietor's a personal brother-in-law of mine …"

"Wagon stickers, wagon stickers, oo'll buy my wagon stickers! Take yer pick from a vast range of light 'earted and witty sayings. Come on, sir, I can see from yer clothes you're a feller with a sense of 'umour …"

"Pies! Pies! Oo'll risk a pie?"

"… Minute I saw you I knew you was a sticker man. Look, 'ere's a good one. My Other Wagon Is A Coach. Or what about my personal favourite — I'm Insured, But Is My Wagon Covered?"

"Carry yer wagon, mate?" growled a deep voice from on high.

Doug looked up and found himself staring up the cavernous nostrils of his first ever giant — a four-metre-tall monster with filed teeth and a shaven head. He was picking between his teeth with what looked like a cricket stump and was using the balcony of somebody's house to scratch the itchy spot between his shoulder blades.

Ruby and Gaffer Naffleton knew the score. They'd seen it all before, and simply stared straight ahead, refusing to be drawn. Doug, however, was overwhelmed. So *this* was how a town was *supposed* to be. For the first time since leaving home, he felt quite light-hearted.

"What's 'appenin'?"

Ray's red face poked through the tarpaulin hanging over the front of the wagon. Several chicken feathers fluttered to the ground.

"We've arrived! We're in Nubb!" Doug told him.

A small, bird-like woman in huge jangly earrings came running up and elbowed her way to the front.

"Tell yer fortune, dearie?" she screeched, grasping Doug's hand. "Cross me palm with silver and Gipsy Gert'll do you a nice one. Listen, beware of violinists who might be on the fiddle…"

"That's enough, Gert, we saw 'im first," said

the sticker man, firmly elbowing her out of the way. "Come on, young man, do yerself a favour, buy a sticker. 'Ow about Please Pass, Run Out Of Horse? Killingly funny, that one."

"Pies! Pies!" screeched the pieman. "Choice o' two delicious fillin's. What'll it be sir? Tripe? Squid 'n' cephalopod?"

"I'll 'ave the tripe," said Ray, reaching into his pocket.

"No you won't," Ruby told him over her shoulder.

"But I'm 'ungry ..." bleated Ray.

Luckily, he was saved from himself. There came a gap in the traffic and Gaffer Naffleton urged the donkeys forward.

"You'll like it at the Conmen, clean sheets every other month ..." cried the foxy-faced goblin persuasively, scuttling alongside.

"One of our most popular lines, this!" howled the sticker man, running behind. "My Other Horse Is Arabian ..."

"Pies!" wailed the pie-seller despondently.

Then, a new voice joined in. It was low and booming, like the hollow sound of an underground river.

"'Ello 'ello 'ello," said the voice. "What's going on 'ere then?"

Suddenly, Doug's new friends were no more. Even the four metre giant. They just trickled away, sucked into the crowd like greasy washing-up water down a drain. You could almost hear the slurp.

Doug turned round, curious to see what could make a four metre giant vanish away without a murmur. The answer was a five metre Troll carrying a truncheon. As far as one could tell (mainly from the fact that she wore earrings) this one was female. Her trunk-like figure sported an ill-fitting outfit of blue serge. She had a rather nasty superfluous weed problem, particularly around the ears, which the earrings and a jaunty little hat did nothing to disguise.

"Having a problem, are we, sir?" she boomed, looming over him.

"Eh? Oh — er — no, no, nothing I can't handle, officer, thank you very much," said Doug, recognising authority when he saw it, even when it was covered with moss and had a small sycamore growing out of its left nostril.

"Glad to hear it, sir. Stranger in these parts, are we?"

"Well yes, actually."

"Thought so," nodded the Troll, looking him over carefully. "If you'll pardon my mentioning it, sir, you have an unusual style of dress. You have a sort of dishevelled, frilly look, sir. Likely to attract the rougher elements, if you know what I mean. Me, for example."

"It's all right, officer, I'm looking after him," chipped in Ruby hastily. "Actually, Doug, Gran doesn't live far from here. it'd probably be quicker if we walk from now on. Thanks for the lift, Gaffer. We'll just untie the horse and be on our way. Come on, Doug. This is where we get off."

Doug couldn't say he was sorry.

CHAPTER THIRTEEN

EVERYONE LIKE FISH?

**Doug and Ray are invited to tea —
Gran Grubb — Some explanations**

Ruby's gran lived up a small cobbled alley leading away from the wharf. Her narrow house was squeezed between two warehouses used, without any shadow of a doubt, for the storing of fish.

A shiny brass plate was mounted on the door, next to a posh bell pull with a gold tassel. It read:

**Mrs Marjory Grubb
Wise Woman to the Stars (genuine)
Please Ring Bell For Appointment**

"I thought you said your granny ran a fish stall," said Doug.

"She does. That's her day job. By night, she's a Wise Woman. Didn't I tell you?"

Ruby pointed to a small piece of paper tacked beneath the posh sign. It read:

CHEAP COD PIECES, FRESH TODAY.
KNOCK AND ASK FOR GRAN.

"Seems a funny combination," observed Doug.

"Why? Fish is supposed to be good for the brain, isn't it?" Ruby said.

"I worked on a fish stall once," Ray reminded them.

"Of course, there's always an exception to every rule," said Ruby cuttingly, and gave the tasselled bell rope a brisk tug. There was a long pause.

"What's happening? Is she out?" Doug wanted to know.

"Just be patient, will you? And don't let the horse drink from that trough. They use it to wash the gutted fish."

Doug and Ray wrestled with the horse, who resisted with some spirit. It was tired. It was stroppy. It had a sore foot. If it wanted to drink fishy water, it would drink fishy water, and that was that.

"Who's that come to see the Wise Woman?" intoned a doomy voice from within.

The door opened, and out stepped Ruby's

granny, muffled from head to foot in her traditional wise woman's hooded cape. She was wiggling her fingers in a mysterious fashion over a crystal ball.

"Hello, Gran," said Ruby.

"Oh, it's you, Rube," said Gran Grubb in a normal voice, pushing her hood back and revealing a cheerful pink face topped with lots of corrugated grey curls. "Well now, int that lovely. Tell the truth, I forgot you was coming, thought it was a punter. Else I wouldn't have gone to the trouble of putting me gear on."

She lowered her voice and peered over Ruby's shoulder. "Who's that there in the funny outfit? And the fat one with spikes?"

"Friends of mine. The blue ragged one is a Moranian prince called Doug. The horse is called Dobbin.* The fat one's Ray. He calls himself a bodyguard, though nobody else does."

"Well now, int that lovely! Prince, eh? Pleased ter meet yer, I'm sure. Tie Dobbin up to the post, and I'll bring him out some hay.** In you come, in you come. I'll fry you up a nice bit of cod for tea."

---

* *The horse's ears pricked up at this. So it was called Dobbin, eh? Well, well. Things were looking up.*

**HAY? *What, that dried yellow stuff? Now they were talking.*

"Is that a new robe, Gran?"

"No, it's the same one, I just swilled it through. Come up nice, dint it? What you got in your basket, Rube?"

"Oh, the usual stuff. Cheese. Elastic. Apples. My bird book. One of Pearl's awful sponges. I had some flowers, but they got a bit squashed …"

"Yes, yes, never mind about that, did you get all them herbs I wanted? Me Creepin' Bindweed? And me Snake Root?"

"Yep. And the Deadly Buglebladder."

"What about me Troll's Trousers?"

"Yep. And the Frog's Napkin. *And* the Old Man's Knee and the Sweaty Bugwort."

"Good girl. I relies on her to get all me bits 'n' bobs what I need from the forest these days. I don't get out there so much as what I did, not now they cut the coaches back," Gran Grubb told Doug and Ray, ushering them into the house. "Come on in, boys. I mean Yer Royal Highness."

"Doug," said Doug. "Just call me Doug."

"Well, come in, whoever you are. And the fat one. You'll 'ave to excuse the mess. These are me workin' quarters."

Gran's working quarters were strictly downmarket. Lots of gloom and carefully strewn rushes and tastefully draped cobwebs. There was a rickety card table and two flimsy chairs. There were sagging shelves full of books with titles like

A Beginner's Guide To Forewarning And Prophecy; *My First Little Weather Forecasting Book*, and, of course, the brilliant *Everything You Always Wanted To Know About Astrology, Horoscopy and Cartomancy But Were Afraid To Pronounce.*

There were tins of tea leaves and packs of playing cards. There were jars of ectoplasm and bundles of dried herbs. There were telescopes, horoscopes, divining rods, crystal balls, candles, almanacs, star charts, calendars, and even a moth-eaten parrot on a perch, who swore under its breath as they went by.

It was all just for effect, of course.

"I keeps it like this for the punters," explained Gran Grubb apologetically. She wasn't sure what sort of decor princes were used to, but she was pretty sure this wasn't it. "They expects it, see."

"It's lovely," Doug reassured her. "Very — er — ominous."

"You really think so?" beamed Gran Grubb. "You don't think I've overdone the cobwebs?"

"Oh, not at all. It's absolutely right. I can just imagine a pointy hat hanging behind the door."

The parrot let out a shrill, sarcastic cackle.

"Actually, I'm not entitled to wear a pointy hat yet. I'm not a Witch, I'm a Wise Woman," Gran Grubb explained. "Not allowed to do the spells, see. Not without the proper certificate. I'm workin' on it, though, ain't I, Rube? Takin' a correspondence course. Never too old, eh? Belt up, Po, or it's parrot pie for supper. Bring your friends out the back, Rube. It's nicer out there."

She pulled aside a piece of old sacking to reveal a cunningly hidden door.

Out the back, there was a comfortable kitchen, which was where Gran Grubb liked to clean fish and relax when she wasn't being Wise. A dozen or more black cats looked up and glared from various benches and baskets as they entered the room. The floor was an obstacle course of saucers of milk and chewed fish heads.

There was a well-scrubbed wooden table and a kettle boiling on a stove. A set of matching cauldrons hung from hooks and a half barrel of ice stood in a corner with fish heads and tails protruding from it.

"See that?" said Gran Grubb, pointing at a damp patch on the ceiling. "I've been on to the council for months about that. But what can I do? I'm only a Wise Woman. 'Ow's yer mum and dad, Rube? And yer sisters? And the baby? Sit down, sit down, I'll get crackin' with the tea. Lay the table, would you, Rube? Everyone like fish?"

"I used to work on a fish stall," Ray told her proudly. He was feeling a lot more cheerful since Ruby had referred to him as a "friend". Even if she did introduce the horse first.

"Well now, int that lovely!" cried Gran Grubb, bustling about with frying pans and chopping blocks while the cats milled about her ankles. "We got summin' in common, then, you 'n' me."

"Perhaps you need an extra hand on your stall, Mrs Grubb?" Doug enquired unkindly. "Ray's got quite a bit of time on his hands ..."

"Oh no, guv. I wouldn't leave you. Not fer all the beetroots in Morania," Ray protested earnestly. "He's only jokin'," he added with an anxious little chuckle.

"How's the correspondence course going then, Gran?" asked Ruby, clattering around with plates and cutlery.

"Not so bad, ducks. I'm enjoyin' the practical. I nearly got that levitation business sorted out. 'Ad Po floatin' up there by the rafters three and a half minutes the other night, I timed it. You should 'ave 'eard what 'e called me when 'e got down. Recipe just needs a bit more dried Throttleweed. 'Ere, you did remember to bring me some, dint you? I been waitin' for that."

"Course I did. Took me three days to find it."

"That's my girl. You can give me a hand tonight after the punters 'ave gone. I need someone to stir while I chant. You boys can 'elp 'n' all."

"Actually, Gran, we have to go out again quite soon. There's something we have to do first. We're on a kind of mission."

"Anything you need my 'elp with? Do I need to wait up?"

"Oh, no, no, nothing I can't handle. I just

promised to help Doug here. He's in a bit of a fix. He's been robbed of a valuable family heirloom. I promised to help him get it back."

"Is that right?" cried Gran Grubb, quivering with sympathy. "Well int that terrible. Sure there's nothin' I can't do to 'elp?"

"Actually, if you've got a cloak or something I can borrow, I'd be grateful," said Doug.

"Of course, of course. You can 'ave this one."

"It's just that this Costume's a bit noticeable."

"I wasn't going to say anything," said Gran Grubb. "But now you mention it …"

"He didn't choose it," Ruby explained fairly. "He was forced to wear it. It's the St Charming's school uniform."

"Oh you don't have to explain things to me. If he's a friend of yours, that's good enough for me."

"Friendship's thicker than wassit," Ray informed her.

"Never a wiser saying," nodded Gran Grubb in agreement. "An' I'm a Wise Woman so I should know. Now. 'Oo wants chips?"

Everyone did.

CHAPTER FOURTEEN

TALENT NITE

Some Real Class Acts — Jester Jangles has a disappointingly poor reception — The arrival of the gang of Princes — Royal Ruin all round — Our heroes discuss their pathetically vague plan of action

"Ladies an' gennelmen, welcome to Talent Nite at The Laughing Footpad!"

There was a murmur of interest, some clapping and a few cheers. The assembled crowd jostled and surged and threw their ale about and picked each other's pockets enthusiastically as Bette Buxom swished her red-satined way to the front of the stage and made her announcement.

The tavern was packed. Terry the bar centaur was rushed off his hooves as eager customers smashed empty tankards down on the puddled counter, howled for peanuts and attempted to rob the specially reinforced till whenever his rump was turned.

"A bit of 'ush, if you please!" bellowed Bette. "Before we start, I'll just run through the 'ouse rules. No booin'. No spittin'. No throwin' stuff. No nickin'. No fightin'. Got that?"

"Booooo!" roared the punters, spitting, throwing sausage rolls and ale around, pocketing each other's wallets and watches and fighting with impunity.

"Right then. Tonight we got some real class acts for you. The Merry Wassailers for a start."

"Boooo!"

"Then there's Big Moll Troll and the Trollettes!"

"Hooray!"

"And over there, in my private booth, we 'ave none other than Mr Popularity 'imself, winner of a dozen Talent Nites, The Singing 'Ighwayman, ladies and gennelmen, who's promised to give us a song later! Say hello, Jacques!"

Jacques Cravat gave his public a morose little wave, then returned to the serious business of drowning his sorrows.

"Oh, boys and gals, 'ave we got treats in store

for you! But first, put your hands together for an old favourite, your own, your very own, Jester Jangles!"

A skinny little chap wearing a red and yellow outfit trimmed with bells got up on stage, braving the hail of boos and sausage rolls as though he did this every day (which, indeed, he did). Ignoring repeated requests to leave the stage, he launched straight into his act. He capered around a bit, then rang his jingling stick and struck a comical pose.

"Marry, sirrahs, hearken to this riddle. I sayeth, I sayeth, I sayeth. Prithee, what do sea monsters eat for tea?"

"Fish and Ships!" yelled the audience, as one.

"Nay!" cried Jester Jangles triumphantly. "That's dinner! For tea they have ferry cakes!"

There was a universal groan, and more sausage rolls bit the dust.

Just then the tavern door burst open, admitting a chilly draught and the sound of high-pitched whinnying.

"I say, chaps, this one's really disgusting! And look, they've got some sort of ghastly local talent thingy going on, what a hoot, haw haw haw. What say we slum it in here, eh wot?"

There was a chorus of braying assent.

"I'm game, Florian. What about you, Ferdinand?"

"Oh rather, Faramond, yah. What a dump, eh? Haw haw."

"What d'you say, Fabius? Shall we go for it?"

"Oh yah. Absolutely. It's divine. So squalid. Super."

"Franz? Fitz? Franklin?"

"Hey, count us in, OK?"

"OK, you guys. Follow me."

In they minced. There were seven of them, which, for a gang of princes, is about right. They all wore the sixth-form version of the St Charming's Costume. This differed from Doug's in several respects. For a start, it was clean and intact. The shirt had an extra frill, and the world-famous hat sported even bigger feathers. The hose were thirty denier with a reinforced gusset. They also had real swords in their scabbards and each had a PREFECT badge pinned to his breast pocket.

Keeping in a tight group, the princes swaggered up to the bar. Terry hastily reached under the counter for his dark glasses. All that glittering gold frogging made his eyes water.

"Well now, yer royal 'ighnessesses, this is an honour. What's it to be?" smiled Terry, showing his yellow teeth and swishing his tail as though he was pleased to see them. Say what you like about princes, they generally turned out to be good tippers.

"Oh. Yah. OK. Whose round is it? Yours, I think, Franz old boy."

"Actually, Florian, old fruit, I think it's yours."

"Really? Oh well, in that case, we'll have a round of that yummy green fizzy stuff with the cherries and the little umbrellas."

"Royal Ruin," nodded Terry, who used to work in an uptown cocktail bar before they fired him for eating all the sugar lumps. "Righty ho, yer royal 'ighnessessesses. Coming right up. Why don't you grab yerselves a table and I'll trot right over with 'em."

Over on the stage, Jester Jangles had been forcibly removed, and three grim dwarfs with accordions who could only have been The Merry Wassailers were setting up their music stands and eyeing up the audience in a menacing way. One was already getting argumentative with a heavy rock fan in the front row, who wanted to see Big Moll Troll and the Trollettes RIGHT NOW.

It looked like it was going to be a good evening.

"Is that it?" asked Doug, staring up doubtfully at The Laughing Footpad. It was slightly set back from the dusty street. A sign hung over the door. It showed a masked man with a large sack over his shoulder running over a rooftop, a triumphant grin on his face. From inside the tavern came the sounds of ribald jeering and breaking glass.

"That's it," nodded Ruby.

"Oh. Right. Er — now what?"

"We'll go in and make discreet enquiries, of course. And do try not to trip over again. We don't want to draw attention to ourselves at this point, all right?"

"I'll try," promised Doug. "It's just that this cloak's about a foot too long. I don't know how your gran walks in it."

"What about me? What am I supposed to do?" whined Ray.

"Stay out here and mind Dobbin," ordered Ruby.

"Why should I?" argued Ray, adding: "I'm a guard. I'm supposed to provide the boss wiv twenty-four hour protection. Don't you worry, Guv. I'll be right behind you."

At that point there was a crash, the tavern door burst open and two grappling figures (one of which was a dwarf) came staggering out and fell to the cobbles. From inside, came the sound of angry voices.

"Actually," said Ray hastily, "actually, perhaps I'll stay out here and mind Dobbin. Just in case we need to make a quick getaway."

CHAPTER FIFTEEN
HELP!

Bette makes an unpopular announcement —
Jacques is still depressed — Terry prepares seven
Royal Ruins — Doug makes discreet enquiries
and gets kidnapped for his trouble — Ruby
locates the rug

The Laughing Footpad on Talent Nite was not the
sort of place where you made discreet enquiries. It
was noisier than a Town Criers' convention, and
any enquiries you made would need to be pitched
somewhere between a workmanlike shriek and an
out-and-out, no-holds-barred primal scream.

"Where's the bar?" howled Doug in Ruby's ear.

"Over there, I think!" Ruby screeched back. "Look, let's separate and see what we can find out. You try the bar. I'm going to snoop about and see what I can see. I'll meet you outside in half an hour."

"What's going on over there? Past the fighting dwarfs with the accordions, look, left of the giant with the hot dog. There's a stage, and a huge woman in red trying to say something through a megaphone …"

But Ruby had already gone.

In fact, Bette Buxom was trying to announce that Big Moll Troll and the Trollettes had withdrawn from tonight's contest owing to a sudden dose of gravel rash.*

It was an unpopular announcement. The audience roared its displeasure and Bette had to give up.

"Cor, it's mad in 'ere tonight all right!" she puffed, collapsing back at her private table where Jacques Cravat sat biting his nails and sulking. "'Ow you feelin' now, Jacques, ducks? More yerself yet?"

The highwayman shook his head, thrust out his underlip and sulked some more.

"Tell you what, why don't you get up and give

---

* One of the more common painful conditions to which Trolls are prone, along with shingles, pumice elbow and subsidence.

'em a song, eh?" coaxed Bette, giving him encouraging little pats on the back. "Cheer yourself up. I mean, let's face it, Jacques, your destiny lies in showbiz. With your looks and talent, you're wasted in the 'ighway robbery business."

"Yeu sink so?"

The tadpoles did a sort of hopeful little dance.

"Certainly I do. Besides, if someone don't go on soon, they'll rip the place apart. They've come to be entertained, an' if anyone can compensate for Big Moll Troll not showin' up, it's you."

Over at the bar, Terry was trying to mix seven Royal Ruins and at the same time catch what was being howled at him by the red-faced youth in the long grey cloak. The cloak looked uncomfortably hot in the oven-like conditions. Terry wondered why the red-faced youth didn't take it off.

"What?" bellowed Terry, busily doing things with cherries. "What d'ya say, mate? Speak up, can't yah?"

"I SAID I'M LOOKING FOR AN OLD FRIEND OF MINE, JACQUES CRAVAT! I'VE BEEN TOLD HE STAYS HERE SOMETIMES!"

"He might do," said Terry guardedly. "Why? You a friend of his, then?"

"OH YES. KNOWN HIM FOR YEARS. WE LEARNT TO RIDE IN THE SAME SADDLE.

OUR MOTHERS WERE BEST FRIENDS. WE'RE PRACTICALLY RELATED!" Doug assured him at the top of his voice.

"Is that so? What's yer name then?" enquired Terry, daintily arranging little paper umbrellas with fingers like salamis.

Doug thought quickly. He didn't move in highwaymen circles. What sort of names did they have? His wildly groping mind suddenly latched on to a half-remembered character from a book he read once.

"DICK TURNIP," he told Terry. "MY FRIENDS CALL ME WILD DICK. YOU MIGHT HAVE HEARD JACQUES SPEAK OF ME. GOOD OLD WILD DICK TURNIP. SOMETHING LIKE THAT."

"Can't say I have," said Terry with a shrug. "But if you want to speak to him, you'll have to wait. He's just about to start his act."

He jerked his thumb in the direction of the stage, where Bette Buxom had again taken up her megaphone. Taken by surprise, Doug whirled round to look.

Unfortunately, someone was treading on Gran Grubb's over-long cloak at the time. The neck fastening snapped and the voluminous garment slid from his shoulders, landing in a grey puddle on the filthy floor. His worse-for-wear, but still gamely-glittering Costume was exposed for all to see.

Doug didn't notice his sudden transformation. He was too busy listening to Bette.

"Ladies and gennelmen, 'ot from 'is world tour, put your 'ands together and give a big Footpad welcome to our very own Singing 'Ighwayman!"

And in true showbiz tradition, Jacques Cravat cast off despair, leapt to his feet and came running on stage, waving and blowing kisses to a cheering audience.

"Merci, mes amis, merci! Ees great to be back in Nubb. For my first song, I seeng for yeu ze beautiful song entitled Ze Singing 'Ighwayman Bleues."

So fascinated was Doug that he didn't really hear the high-pitched whinnying coming from just behind him.

"Well, well, well," trilled the voice. "Now, what do we have here? Tell me, chaps, do my eyes deceive me, or is that beastly little unwashed brat wearing our glorious Costume?"

"You're right, Florian. Probably a nasty little wet-behind-the-ears, new-boy-type thingy. Playing truant, eh what? What d'you think, Ferdinand?"

"Looks ripe for bullying to me. I say we get him and rough him up a bit then take him back to school and get Spittoon to stick him in Detention! What say you?"

"Yah, yah, let's get him!"

"Help!" cried Doug, finding himself surrounded by seven glittering princes with their swords drawn.

But nobody did.

Meanwhile, Ruby crouched in the middle of Bette Buxom's private sitting room, feeding the last of Bette's chocolates to the small fluffy dogs and staring thoughtfully at the tattered rug on the floor. It was unmistakably Doug's precious missing heirloom all right. It was the only shabby item in the room. It looked pathetically out of place.

Far away in the distance she could hear a voice coming through several thicknesses of wall.

"I got zose Ride Out In A Rush again,
'Ide Be'ind A Bush again
Rob A Coach At Peestol Point Bleues,"
Jacques Cravat was singing.

There was another sound too. Feet coming down the passageway.

"Help!" muttered Ruby.

Quick as a flash, she made for the window.

At exactly the same time as Ruby was scrambling through the back window, Doug was being hustled through the front door of The Laughing Footpad and into a waiting coach by the gang of princes. There was a great deal of sword-waving and swaggering and malicious laughter.

Outside, Ray was leaning against the horse chewing a hot dog which he'd bought from a passing street vendor. His mouth dropped open in alarm as he recognised the victim.

"Oi!" he shouted without really thinking. "Oi! Whatchoo playin' at?"

The tallest and most glittery prince heard.

"Did you want something, fellow?" he enquired coldly.

"Oh no," said Ray. "Nuthin' at all, sir. Mistaken wassit. Identity. Thort I knew 'im but I don't. 'Ave a nice day."

And he bit into his hot dog and tried to chew unconcernedly as Doug was bundled into a waiting coach.

"St Charming's," snapped the tallest and most glittery prince. "And step on it!"

The coachman cracked his whip and the coach went tearing off down the road and screeched around the corner in a cloud of dust.

At that moment, Ruby came running from the back of the building.

"I've found it!" she was shouting. "I know where the rug is! Have you seen Doug?"

"Help!" muttered Ray to himself. "Now I'm really for it."

Altogether, not a very successful evening.

Gran Grubb at work — Ruby reports back —
Some interesting information about
Hartustandi rugs

"He was what?" said Gran Grubb, looking up from her cauldron, startled.

"Shanghaied," said Ruby, putting a saucepan of milk on to boil. "Kidnapped. Forcibly abducted and carted off to St Charming's by a pressgang of thuggy princes. Where d'you keep the cocoa?"

"Well I never. That's no way to treat royalty," remarked Gran Grubb, peering at her recipe book. "Some people got no respect. Top shelf, right-hand side. While you're up there, fetch down a jar of dried ferret fingers, there's a good girl."

"It was royalty who did it, Gran. Actually, I didn't see it happen. I was too busy looking for his precious rug at the time. I think you're out of ferret fingers."

"No I'm not, I got some somewhere. 'Is precious what?"

"Rug. Some tatty old lump of carpet he reckons is a valuable family heirloom. Jacques Cravat stole it from him. We were trying to get it back."

"Oh, really? Antique carpet, eh? Did he say where it's from?"

"Er … now, where was it again? Something about not being able to get up. Hard to rise? Hard to get up …?"

"'Artustand?" cried Gran Grubb eagerly, forgetting to stir in her excitement. "Are you telling me your friend Doug's got a genuine 'Artustandi rug?"

"Well, he *had* one. He hasn't got it now."

"So you didn't find it?"

"Yes, yes, I found it. It was in Bette Buxom's sitting room, but I got disturbed."

"Oh," said Gran, sounding disappointed. "Now, that *is* a pity. So what 'appened?"

"So I had to escape out a window and climb down a drainpipe. Then, after all that, I find that idiot Ray has gone and let Doug be kidnapped.

He actually watched it happen. The pair of them can't be trusted on their own for a single second. Especially Ray. Ah, here's the ferret fingers."

"Shush," scolded Gran Grubb, taking the jar and adding a handful to the brew simmering in the cauldron. She had developed a soft spot for Ray, on account of his fishy background. "Don't you be so 'ard on Ray. I'm sure he did 'is best. 'E's just not cut out for bodyguardin', that's 'is trouble. Where's he now? I expect 'e's ready for a bite o' supper. I can do 'im a nice bowl o' fish soup."

"Well, he won't be needing it tonight. I left him in an alley opposite the Laughing Footpad with strict instructions to follow anyone who leaves with a rug under their arm."

"What, an' you're gonna leave 'im there? On 'is own? All night?"

"Well, he's got Dobbin with him," said Ruby defensively. "I can't do much now, can I? I'll sort out everything tomorrow morning. Right now, I'm too tired. I want to go to bed. It's exhausting, doing all the thinking for everybody."

Gran added a pinch of Troll's Trousers to her brew and stirred thoroughly. "I feel sorry for that Dobbin," she remarked. "I dunno why you drag it round all the time."

"It's sure to come in useful sooner or later. Look, why did you get so excited about Doug's rug? What's so special about Hartustandi rugs anyway?"

"Well, they're worth a fortune, ain't they?" said Gran Grubb.

"Are they?"

Ruby thought back to Doug's shabby old rug, spread out like an abandoned dishcloth on Bette's floor.

"But Doug's rug looks like something that fell off a rag-and-bone cart."

"That's as maybe. But 'Artustandi rugs never was particularly famed for their beauty."

"So what are they famed for?"

"They fly," said Gran simply.

"What? Really? You mean, up in the air? Are you sure?"

"Certainly I am. I'm a Wise Woman, remember? I move in magic circles. Give me a bit of credit."

"Well I never," said Ruby. "Doug never mentioned it. I wonder if he knows?"

"Shouldn't think so. Comin' from a backwater like Morania. An' even if he did, I don't suppose he believes it. Not unless he's had a go. People never believe in flying carpets till they've had a go. An' you can understand it really. I mean, you don't see a lot of 'em round these days. Shouldn't be surprised if that rug of Doug's weren't the only one left in the world. Well, well. An 'Artustandi rug. 'Course, only certain people can make it work."

"Ah. I thought there might be a snag. What sort of people?"

"People who know the word for "up" in 'Artustandi."

"Do you?" asked Ruby.

"Not offhand. But I could look it up. There's a book I got sure to 'ave it in."

"So let me get this straight. Doug's rug is a flying carpet worth a fortune. Right?"

"Right. If 'e sold it on the open market, it'd fetch a king's ransom."

"In which case Morania would be saved and he wouldn't have to go to St Charming's," mused Ruby, sipping her cocoa.

"Right."

"He'll be pleased about that," said Ruby.

"I bet 'e will. 'Ere, changing the subject, 'ow was the talent contest? I don't get along there so much since I started the correspondence course."

"Rubbish," Ruby told her. "You didn't miss a thing."

"Jacques Cravat there, then, was he?"

"He certainly was. After what he did to Doug, he's got a real nerve to get up and sing. Talk about conceited."

"Got a nice voice, though," said Gran.

Josiah T. Whiplash, Headmaster — Henry
Spittoon, Hall Porter — Prince Florian gives his
report — Doug is interrogated with dire
consequences

The name on the door said JOSIAH T.
WHIPLASH (M. Ad. Hons) — but nobody
called him anything but Headmaster. (Except in
private, when they called him a lot of things.)*

Nobody knew how old he was, but his particular

---

*Some of them were a lot worse than Mr
Whippy.*

style of enlightened leadership owed a lot to the Stone Age. His school of thought believed that there wasn't much that a great deal of apoplectic screeching followed by a good thrashing couldn't fix. That was just fine with the parents, who, being royal, believed in traditional methods.

Right now, Josiah was confined to his Bath chair with a nasty ingrowing toenail. That, combined with the disappointing result of the inter-school under elevens fencing contest (Knickerbockers 28 – St Charming's 0) had put him in an even worse temper than usual. He sat in his study with a plaid blanket pulled up to his chin. A cane lay across his lap. His eyes smouldered hotly from beneath a pair of wildly-sprouting eyebrows which, together with jungly side-whiskers, looked set to colonise his face.

"Exactly when and where do you say this young whelp was picked up?" he rumbled.

"Late last night hin one of them low life taverns down by the docks, 'Eadmaster. 'E was spotted and happrehended by young Prince Florian 'ere," the hall porter informed him with relish.

The hall porter's name was Henry Spittoon and he wore a red greatcoat adorned with dozens of brass buttons. On his head was a tricorn hat and on his large feet were steel-capped shoes. He always carried a truncheon, and on his belt hung a massive keyring. Next to him stood Prince Florian, inspecting his horsey teeth in a hand mirror.

"And what were you doing down by the docks, lad?" Josiah Whiplash barked, beetling and seething away.

"Oh, the usual, Headmaster," Florian hastened to explain. "It was the prefects' night out. We were having lots of jolly fun. Overturning barrows. Whistling at lavender girls. Pushing shoeshine boys around. Swaggering and making offensive remarks in loud voices. You would have been proud of us, sir."

Spittoon gave an approving nod.

"No cause for complaint there, 'Eadmaster. Perfectly hacceptable be'aviour Hi'd say."

Josiah T. Whiplash looked unconvinced.

"Hmm. Did you throw food around in restaurants and generally upset your fellow diners with your unspeakably bad manners and loutish behaviour?"

"Of course, Headmaster. That goes without saying," said Prince Florian smugly, smoothing a moistened finger over a haughty eyebrow.

"Did you kick any stray dogs?"

"Loads, Headmaster."

"Did you jump in any fountains? Draw moustaches on any statues? Frighten any horses? Terrorise any old ladies?"

"We certainly did, Headmaster. And Franz

upset a dustbin. Terrible mess, all over the jolly old road."

"That's all right then," rumbled Josiah with grudging approval. "Wouldn't like to feel you were letting the school down. We have a reputation to keep up. Now, tell me. What first attracted your attention to this young rapscallion in the first place?"

"Oh, without a doubt, the shocking state of his Costume, Headmaster. It was as though he jolly well couldn't care less what he looked like. I doubt whether he's ever heard of fabric softener. Really letting the side down, you know? We were jolly horrified, I can tell you."

Prince Florian shuddered at the thought, and dabbed at his nose with a scented hanky.

"Hmm. All right, lad, get out. Run along to harpsichord class, or wherever it is you're supposed to be. Well, come on, Spittoon, what are you waiting for? Wheel the young varmint in and let's hear what he's got to say for himself."

Doug was sitting on a hard bench in the corridor. His right ankle was manacled to a handy ring set in the wall. He was so tired he could hardly keep his eyes open, having spent the night in Detention. This meant being chained up and dripped on in St Charming's private dungeon, which had nothing more going for it than a state-run dungeon except a better class of rat.

His Costume was by now little more than a

collection of old rags. His hat had lost all but one of the original feathers. He had lost a shoe in the scuffle of the night before. His mock sword was bent. His knees poked through his hose. He had had nothing to eat since Gran Grubb's fried cod the day before. There was no doubt about it. Things just weren't going well for him.

At the end of the passageway, past a tall suit of armour reverently labelled OUR NOBLE FOUNDER, a leaded window overlooked a playing field where a number of puffed-out small boys clad in the Costume were hobbling around the running track. Each carried a glass shoe on a slippery red cushion.

Beyond the playing field, behind the stables, a first year jousting tournament was taking place. Pennants flapped in the breeze, and you could hear distant clangs as small riders tumbled off their horses and were dragged off screaming to the sanatorium.

Doug started as the door flew open and the chief bully from the night before, the one they called Florian, minced out and smirked unpleasantly before strutting off down the corridor. Immediately after him came the hall porter with the buttons and the truncheon and the steel-capped shoes. The one they called Spittoon. The one who had put him in Detention the night before and locked the door on him.

Importantly, Spittoon selected a key, stooped

down and unlocked Doug's manacle.

"Hin," said Spittoon, dragging him to his feet and giving him a spiteful push. "The 'Eadmaster wants to see you."

Hin reeled Doug, to find himself confronted by a demented-looking ancient in a Bath chair who looked as though he ate hot coals for breakfast.

So this was him. Mr Whippy. Josiah T. Whiplash, Headmaster, M. Ad. Hons, whose feared name still caused a nervous frown to crease his father's brow thirty years on. Looking at him, Doug could understand why. He radiated anger. He made you want to run gibbering into a corner crying for your mum.

"How d'you do, sir," said Doug, giving a little bow.

"Don't try that on with me, sonny!" shrieked Josiah T. Whiplash, thrashing about him with his cane. "Don't try that tone of voice with me! Think I was born yesterday?"

Doug wisely decided not to answer. To try and calm his nerves, he took a deep breath and looked around the room. For a collector of antiques, Mr Whippy's study was extremely austere. Apart from the desk, a globe, some bookshelves, a mounted display of canes and some sort of stuffed rodent in a glass case, the room was empty.

"Name?" lashed Josiah T. Whiplash.

"Prince Douglas of Morania," said Doug promptly.

"Morania? Morania? Damp cesspit to the north? Nobody ever goes there and quite right too?"

"That's it," said Doug. "It's the bit on the map where it's marked HERE BE BEETROOTS."

"Ruled by an empty-headed king name of Donald? Hopeless at kingdom management? Fond of the gee-gees? Plays a lot of cards? Married a hairdresser named Deirdre or something?"

"That's Dad," agreed Doug with an affectionate little smile. "That's him all right."

"I remember him. Never forget a name. Young Donald. Brain like soup in a colander. Failed everything. Expelled him for gambling in the finish. Remember Donald of Morania, Spittoon?"

"Before my time, 'Eadmaster."

"Consider yourself lucky. So. You're the spawn, eh? And what might you be doing cavorting around inns wearing this disgraceful mockery of a Costume?"

"Funnily enough, I was on my way here," Doug told him. "At least, I intended to get here eventually. It's a long story."

"Make it quick," advised Josiah T. Whiplash.

Doug thought for a moment, composing his thoughts.

"Well," he said. "When I started off, my Costume was quite respectable. Not my choice, you understand, but I looked reasonably smart. I had a coach, a horse, a driver, a bodyguard, some luggage, a bag of gold, a valuable family heirloom and a Letter Of Introduction from Dad. Sadly, I was the victim of a robbery, and …"

"This is taking too long," broke in Josiah T. Whiplash. "Can you pay the fees? Answer yes or no."

"Well, no, not exactly …"

"I thought not. Like father like son. He never had a penny to his name either. This is a school, lad, not a charity institution. Spittoon, take him along to Matron and tell her to incarcerate him in the san while I decide what to do with him."

"What? Now, hold on just a minute …"

"Hear that? Just like his father. Take a hundred lines for insolence. I WILL NOT ANSWER MY HEADMASTER BACK. In by four o'clock on the dot. Got that?"

"But …"

"What's that, boy? Still complaining? D'you want to go back in Detention?"

Henry Spittoon's fingers began to twitch and he looked hopeful.

"Lead me to Matron," said Doug.

CHAPTER EIGHTEEN

AT LOOSE IN CHARMING'S

**Threatened by Matron — Escape — Running
— A nasty stitch — A dancing class in progress
— Mrs Plunket and Mr Plumfairy**

"Who's a grubby boy, then?" cooed Matron,
advancing with a wet flannel. Tucked under
one stout arm was a huge bottle of medicine. A
spoon, a spatula and a seriously sharp pair of
scissors protruded from her top pocket. A
thermometer was stuck behind her ear. "Who's a
naughty little mucky pup? Who's been playing in
the muddy puddles and got his Costume all torn
and dirty?"

"Look, do you mind," said Doug, backing away.

He didn't like the look of the sanatorium. It reminded him of having his appendix out, years ago in Morania. Something to do with the barred windows, perhaps, and the smell of disinfectant and cabbage water.

And Matron, of course.

She had him trapped between two long rows of starched beds. Several contained small, heavily-bandaged patients who stared interestedly from white pillows as the drama unfolded.

"What we gonna do with him, eh? What we gonna do with him?" beamed Matron, rolling ever onward and waving an admonishing finger. "What we gonna do with his dirty little chubby chops? We're gonna give him a big, big wash, that's what we're gonna do. A big, big scrub-a-dub-dub."

"I can do it myself," Doug told her, desperately looking for an escape route. She was blocking his route to the only door. He now knew how a hedgehog must feel in the path of an approaching coach and four. "Really. I know how."

"And then," continued Matron, taking the thermometer from behind her ear and shaking it vigorously — "and then we're going to take his temperature and give him a big dose of nasty medicine and find him some lovely clean jimjams and give him some nice din-dins and then he's going to bye-byes."

"No he's not. I mean, no I'm not. Not possible. Sorry. Look, the Headmaster wants a hundred lines in by four o'clock."

"Not till we've washed those handy pandies and taken our medicine and said hello to Mr Sandman," said Matron firmly.

She was almost upon him. Doug panicked. He knew hospital routine. In another moment she would have him by the scruff of his ruff, and then it would just be a matter of time before he was scrubbed, polished, dosed, threatened with a bedpan, strapped into a bed and force-fed slimy boiled fish and lumpy mashed potato followed by lukewarm semolina pudding, all washed down with a cup of weak tea.

The situation called for desperate action.

"Look behind you!" screeched Doug, pointing at a spot on the floor just behind Matron's sensible shoes. "Yuck! Isn't that just the biggest spider you've ever seen?"

It was corny, and it was a gamble — but Doug knew a bit about gambling. He wasn't his father's son for nothing.

"Eeeek!" squawked Matron, just as he had hoped, and she leapt up on the nearest bed. From the howl of pain, Doug guessed that it contained an unlucky patient — but he didn't wait to find out for sure. In seconds he had bolted up the narrow passageway between the beds and was out of the door, where the air smelled fresh and there wasn't a bowl of grapes or a bottle of Lucozade to be seen. There was a winding gravel path that went around the corner. Goodness knows where it would lead him, but anywhere was preferable than back to Matron.

It led past a number of long, low out-buildings in which various classes were taking place. If any of the second years taking Studies In Architectural Criticism with Old Crusty in the science block had happened to have been a) awake and/or b) looking out of the window at that particular moment, they might have been surprised to see a wild-looking apparition, wearing torn blue rags and only one shoe, flash past.

On ran Doug — past classes in Princely Deportment, Banquet Etiquette, Butler Baiting and Peasant Patronising; past lessons in Dealing With Ungracious Grooms and Coping With Cocky Gardeners. Past Posing For Portraits and Looking Good Whilst Hunting. Past Archery, Falconry, and Waving From Balconies.

On, on, past dormitories and laboratories. Past the stables, where sweating horses were having their tournament paraphernalia removed by ungracious grooms. Past well-stocked flowerbeds and rolling lawns, tended by cocky gardeners. Past the fencing area, where the third years were preparing for their grade three fencing exam, so that they could finally hang up their mock swords and wave around the real thing; past the dining hall, where teams of chefs were preparing trays of food for the princes to throw about and smear in each other's hair in true upper-class fashion — past yet more classrooms.

And then he stopped, because he was all puffed out and developing the beginnings of a very nasty stitch.

Where he stopped was in front of the gymnasium, where there was a ballroom-dancing class in progress. The gym was built along the lines of a summerhouse, with huge glass doors overlooking the playing field. Inside, polished wooden floors squeaked protestingly under the combined weight of a hundred or more shuffling left feet belonging to fifty or so pairs of princes, all arguing about whose turn it was to lead.

The class was presided over by a small, dapper, twinkled-toed master in shiny shoes. A cascading wig of golden curls tumbled to his shoulders and in his hand he held a silver cane, which he used to beat both time and ankles. He had the daintiest, pointiest little feet you ever saw.

Over in a dark corner, behind the vaulting horse, a very old lady with a wispy grey bun sat at a tinny harpsichord banging out a waltz.

"One, two, three!" trilled the dancing master, lashing about with his stick. "Pick your feet up, gentlemen, if you please! And nice big smiles, eh? We must try and look as if we are enjoying ourselves, mustn't we? From the top, Mrs Plunket, if you please."

But the very old lady was staring over her half-glasses, over the harpsichord and out the window at a wild, ragged-looking youth who had collapsed against a nearby tree, clutching his side and gasping for breath.

"I don't know who that boy is, Mr Plumfairy," observed Mrs Plunket, pointing a disapproving finger, "but whoever he is, he's late."

**Ray awakens and speaks of his
uncomfortable night — Ruby is
unsympathetic — Possibilities are discussed
and discarded — Bette and the rug emerge**

"It's about bloomin' time you showed up,"
remarked Ray bitterly, struggling to a sitting
position and wringing the morning dew from his
balaclava. "I bin 'ere all night I 'ave. What time is
it?"

"Five o'clock in the morning."

"Where you bin?"

"In bed, sleeping," said Ruby.

"Well, that's nice I muss say. You goes 'ome to bed while me 'n' Dobbin spends a night out 'ere on the cobbles. Perishin' it was. I coulda caught me death. An' I'm starvin'."

"Gran said you would be. She made you some fish-paste sandwiches."

"Yeah? Where are they, then?"

"In the kitchen. I forgot them."

"YOU WHAT?"

"Oh, stop complaining. You're a guard, aren't you?" said Ruby, taking some sugar lumps out of her basket and feeding them to the horse. "Isn't that what guards do? Stand to attention all night and shoot anything that moves?"

"That's sentries," explained Ray. "I'm a personal bodyguard. That's more like a mate, reelly. I can't believe you forgot them sarnies."

"Some mate," said Ruby. "Let him get shot at and robbed and then captured. Some mate."

"Well, I am so," insisted Ray. "We bin through a lot together, me an' the guv. 'E's only jokin' when 'e talks about firin' me. You don't wanna take no notice o' that. That's just 'is sense o' wassit. Me an' 'im's very close reelly. Let's 'ave one o' them sugar lumps."

"No chance. So did you see anything? No sign of Jacques Cravat?"

"Not a thing. A few fights at chuckin' out time, then dead as a wassit."

Ruby looked across at The Laughing Footpad.

It had a very closed, early-morningish, not-at-home-to-callers sort of air, with definitely drawn shutters and a firmly barred and bolted door.

"Good. That means the rug must still be in there. Incidentally, Gran thinks there's a good chance it's a genuine flying carpet, and worth a fortune. Might even be the only one left in the world."

"Gerroff. Reelly?" said Ray, round-eyed.

"Really. Now all we've got to do is go in there and get it out."

There was a short pause.

"How?" asked Ray.

"Oh, there's loads of ways. You just don't have any imagination, do you, Ray? I can't think why we're lumbered with you on this adventure, you're completely useless."

"No I'm not," argued Ray.

"Yes you are. You haven't a clue how to set about getting the rug back, have you?"

"Well, what about you, then? You got any ideas?" challenged Ray.

"Hundreds," Ruby told him airily.

"Like what?"

"Well, for a start we could try the New Rugs For Old routine. With a bell and cart."

"We 'aven't got a bell," Ray pointed out triumphantly.

"All right then, here's another one. I could disguise myself as a serving wench come to clean the rooms and smuggle it out under my apron."

"Loada rubbish. It wouldn't fit."

"All right then, how about this? You break the door down, go to where Jacques Cravat is sleeping, kick his door in, show him your spiky thing on a chain and insist that he gives the rug back this minute. And everything else he took. With an apology."

There was a long silence while Ray thought about this.

"Any other ideas?" he asked, after a bit.

"Millions. But what was wrong with the last one?"

"Well," said Ray. "It's not that I'm scared or anything. It's just that I don't trust meself. After what 'e did to the guv. I might run amok or summin'. An' someone's got to stay wiv Dobbin 'ere. An' besides ..."

"What? Why arc you going red?"

"I left me spiky thing on a chain at your gran's," admitted Ray sheepishly. But Ruby wasn't listening. She was staring intently across the road at The Laughing Footpad.

"Shhh," she said. "Get back. Something's happening."

The door opened, and out came Bette Buxom wearing a black, hooded cloak trimmed with scarlet feathers. In one hand she carried a large black handbag. Under her arm, she had a long, floppy brown paper parcel.

Cautiously, with an air of great secrecy, she looked up and down the road.

"The rug!" breathed Ruby. "She's taking it somewhere. She must have a customer lined up already. I wonder who?"

At this point, a small carriage pulled by a shaggy pony came hurtling around the corner and screeched to a halt. The driver leapt down to open the door and attempted to assist Bette with her parcel.

"Get yer grubby hands off!" snapped Bette, giving him a shove which sent him reeling into the gutter. She hugged her prize to her ample bosom. "This is valuable, this is. I'll take care of it if it's all the same to you. Stand back."

She threw the rug in and clambered in after it. The driver staggered back to the coach, dragged himself up into his seat, clicked his tongue — and away they went.

"Now what?" asked Ray.

"We follow, of course. What d'you think the horse is for?" said Ruby briskly, climbing on to a low wall and getting astride Dobbin's broad back.

"But what about the guv?"

"Rug first, Doug later. Get on, or I'm going without you. Right, Dobbin, now's your chance to prove yourself. Follow that cab!"

CHAPTER TWENTY

THIS YOU'RE GOING TO LIKE

A meeting between Bette and Mr Whippy —
Josiah tries his hand at flattery — Bette's sales
pitch — A sale is agreed — Doug has a run-in
with Frederick of Mushcatoon

"My dear, dear lady. What a delightful surprise!"
burbled Josiah T. Whiplash. "Come in, come in,
do! Dust off the chair for the lady, Spittoon.
Where are your manners? Forgive me for not
rising, dearest madam, I fear I'm suffering from a
rather painful ingrowing toenail. May I offer you
a drink?"

He whipped off his mortar board and cupped it over his heart.

"Ooooh, tee hee, nice to see you again Headmaster, hope you don't mind me callin' in on the off chance, only summink's just come in and the minute I seen it I thought of you. I'll sit 'ere shall I. Yes please, a sweet sherry," cooed Bette, plumping down gratefully on a chair and laying her parcel carefully across her lap.

"Ah, of course, of course, dear lady, I remember, sweet sherry it shall be although of course you're sweet enough already, ha, ha," smarmed Josiah T. Whiplash. "A sweet sherry for the fair lady, if you please, Spittoon, and a glass of port for myself."

"Right haway, 'Eadmaster!" said Henry Spittoon, walking to the wall and pressing a small button which caused a secret panel to slide to one side, revealing a well-stocked drinks cabinet.

"Make it snappy, Spittoon! We mustn't keep Beauty waiting."

"Oooh, Headmaster!" simpered Bette.

"Oh yes, indeed. May I say what a charming sight you are to a plain old bachelor like me," drooled Josiah.

"Oooh, Headmaster, you know just what to say to a girl," tittered Bette, pushing back her hood and patting her sausage curls.

"No, no, I mean it. You are the Rose In The Desert."

"Ooh, Headmaster!"

"You are the Ray Of Sunshine In The Dark Dungeon," continued Josiah T. Whiplash, as Spittoon set two glasses on the desk before them and proceeded to pour.

"Oh my!"

"You are the Pearl In The Oyster. That'll be all, Spittoon, get out and see that we're not disturbed."

Spittoon gave a little salute, clicked his heels together and obediently left the room.

"Now then, dear lady, where were we?"

"You was buttering me up with your honeyed words, Headmaster, you naughty flatterer!"

"So I was, so I was. You are — erm — the Dollop Of Jam In A Stale Doughnut."

It wasn't easy to come up with these. Josiah was having to think a bit now.

"Oooh, tee hee, you're so poetic, Headmaster, say another one!"

"You are ... you are the Bowl Of Pot Pourri In The Toilet," Josiah T. Whiplash produced triumphantly.

Bette wasn't so sure about that one. Her smile faded.

"Have a drink," he said hastily, thrusting a glass into her hand. "To us, madam, and the continued success of our business partnership."

"'Ere's mud in yer eye," agreed Bette, and downed her sherry in one. Josiah T.

Whiplash leant forward eagerly.

"Now then, my dearest, dearest lady, to business. What have you brought to tempt me today?"

His hot, hard, greedy little eyes bored into the paper parcel lying limply on Bette's lap.

"Ah," said Bette, setting down her glass and suddenly becoming much more businesslike. "Now then, Headmaster, this you're going to like. This is you, this is. I was very lucky to get hold of one of these, I can tell you. I 'ave it on good authority it come from a royal palace."

"Yes, yes, but what is it?" cried Josiah T. Whiplash, well into Mad Collector mode now, hardly able to contain himself. "What is this priceless treasure you've brought to add to my collection?"

"Hang about, I'm just undoin' this last knot … there. That's got it."

Bette ripped off the last of the paper, stood, shook out Doug's rug and spread it carefully on the floor.

"Look at that. A genuine antique Hartustandi rug!" announced Bette. "What d'you think? Lovely, ain't it? Looks nice on yer floorboards, don't it? Really sets 'em off."

Josiah T. Whiplash couldn't see it. Being a mad collector, he was used to forcing himself to see beauty in the ugliest of objects. Indeed, behind another secret panel to the right of the bookshelves lurked an entire room chock-full of ghastly paintings, boring stamp collections, rusty suits of armour, carriage clocks, toby jugs, ancient coach lamps and onyx ashtrays. With an effort, he could see merit in all of them. But Doug's rug had him beat.

"It's got a certificate," enthused Bette, reaching into her bosom and fishing it out. "See? There, look. Made in Hartustand. Genuine. Hand-woven. See?"

"Hrmmmm."

Josiah reached into his pocket and produced a pair of pince-nez which he wedged beneath his gigantic eyebrows. He took the certificate and examined it. Then, frowning, he peered down at the rug.

"I can't quite — to be absolutely frank, it looks rather — I don't — is it — er?"

"What, you never heard of Hartustandi carpets? I'm surprised at you, Headmaster. An' you a connoisseur of rare and beautiful things. Well, you can take it from me, there won't be any other collectors with one of these in their possession, I can tell you. The Book says there's only three left in the world. That means it's almost unique — apart from two others, both in private collections. Terrible sought after, Hartustandi rugs."

"Really?"

Josiah broke out in a sweat. He could imagine

springing this upon his fellow mad collectors at the next Mad Collectors Annual Reunion Luncheon. He imagined them going green and foaming at the mouth with envy. ("I say, chaps, have you seen what old Whippy's got his hands on? Genuine Hartustandi rug, of all things. Lucky bounder.") Only three in the world, eh?

But, somehow ... those nasty stains ... those dog hairs ...

"Why?" he asked humbly. "Why are Hartustandi rugs terribly sought after?"

There was a pause.

"Well, it's the craftsmanship, ain't it?" said Bette. "The colours and that. The pattern. Why, you only got to look at the weave ..."

She was doing her best, but faced with Doug's rug she couldn't help sounding uncertain.

Josiah remained unconvinced. He fiddled worriedly with his side whiskers.

"Hmm. Would you say those are poodles? Two poodles fighting over a bone, do you think? Or crocodiles being sick in a bucket? And is that meant to be a flower? Or has somebody dropped a plateful of beetroot? That blob over there looks suspiciously like ..."

"Poodles, flowers, beetroot, who cares?" cried Bette. "I dunno. Why's anythin' anythin'? It's all a matter o' taste. 'Course, they do say ..."

She gave a little titter.

"They do say Hartustandi carpets can fly. But

personally I reckon that's just a rumour. Livin' in Nubb, I reckon I seen most things — but I ain't never seen a flyin' carpet. Trolls 'n' giants 'n' witches 'n' centaurs I can take, but a flyin' carpet's flyin' against nature, ain't it? No, I reckon it's all down to the quality of the craftsmanship. The beautiful colours an' ... the er ... the lovely stitchin'." Again she trailed off and her eyes flickered doubtfully to the tired old rag on the floor.

"Ah, what the heck. How should I know what's so flippin' good about it? Carpets ain't really my line. Anyway, if *What Rug* says it's valuable, that's good enough for me."

"It's just so — you know," said Josiah weakly. "Tacky."

"Oh, well, of course I'm not saying it don't need a bit of a clean up," said Bette, sounding a bit huffy. "I mean, you wouldn't look in mint condition if someone 'ad walked over you for two 'undred years. Anyway, if you don't want it ..."

And she made to roll it up.

Josiah broke.

"Oh, but I do, I do! Tell, me dear lady, how much?" he cried, reaching into his robe for his wallet.

"More than what you got in there," said Bette with a greedy gleam in her eye.

Down in the gymnasium, Doug and his partner

stumbled around hopelessly and tried not to crash into other dancing couples.

"COUNT, gentlemen, COUNT!" instructed Mr Plumfairy, lashing about him with his stick. "One, two, three, one, two, three. Listen to the music, straight backs, let's point our toes, shall we? And let's try not to fight our partners, gentlemen. This is ballroom dancing, not all-in wrestling!"

"I think he's talking to you," remarked Doug's partner nastily. "That's the third time you've stepped on my foot."

"Good," said Doug. He had taken an instant dislike to his partner, whose name was Prince Frederick of Mushcatoon. Frederick had a particularly haughty air and flaring nostrils, and made no secret of the fact that the last person in the world he would voluntarily choose to dance with would be Doug.

"My father's an emperor, you know," snarled Prince Frederick of Mushcatoon into Doug's ear. "He doesn't pay two hundred gold pieces a term to have my toes trampled by squalid down-and-outs from tinpot countries who can't even keep their Costumes tidy."

"I know what you mean," said Doug, whirling him into a corner and kicking him sharply on the ankle.

"Aaah!" screamed Prince Frederick, clutching his foot and falling to the floor. "He attacked me!

Sir, sir! Please, sir! The new boy just attacked me!"

"All right, all right, break it up. Stop, Mrs Plunket, if you please. You over there! New boy! What d'you think you're doing?"

"I'm beating up my dancing partner," Doug explained pleasantly. "Do please carry on with the music, Mrs Plunket, this won't take long."

Shocked muttering spread amongst the dancers. Beating up one's partner evidently wasn't done, especially if you were a new boy who didn't take care of your Costume.

"Well, don't," Mr Plumfairy told him irritably. "It's not good manners. Duels at dawn. That's how princes settle arguments, not on the dance floor. You've got to take these classes seriously. Supposing it was a real princess you were dancing with? Then what?"

"Actually, I'm the girl. He's leading," said Doug, pointing at his partner, who was writhing around on the floor weeping.

"Don't argue, lad. Take a hundred lines. I Will Not Fight In Dancing Class. Right. If you're ready, gentlemen? Take your partners for the paso doble. Take it away, Mrs Plunket!"

Mrs Plunket struck up a vaguely exotic rhythm on her harpsichord, and the assembled princes sorted themselves into pairs. Prince Frederick gave Doug a furious glare and limped into the changing rooms.

For the first time in his life, Doug found out what it was like to be a wallflower.

It wasn't so bad.

CHAPTER TWENTY-ONE

YOU CAN'T TRUST NOBODY

Ruby listens, learns and leaps into action —
A break-in — The rug regained — Ruby tries to
speak Hartustandi and is disturbed —
Airborne at last!

Ruby stood motionless in the shadow of the
Noble Founder's suit of armour and waited until
the porter's receding footsteps were no more. She
then nipped back to her previous position, with
her ear clamped, limpet fashion, against the
Headmaster's study door.

From inside came the sound of muffled voices. Despite straining her ears to their limits, she couldn't quite hear what was being said over the general background of school noises: the far-off, resigned chanting of the eight times table; the clash of steel from the fencing yard; the distant bawl of an irate master; the squeak of chalk on a blackboard; the tinny tinkle of a harpsichord playing, of all things, a paso doble. It was most frustrating.

Apart from one small incident where she almost got spotted by a gardener's boy when climbing through a window, and another where she nearly got trampled by a geography class, Ruby had found it pitifully easy to trail Bette Buxom through the maze of corridors as far as the Head's room. She hadn't even needed a piece of elastic.

In fact, her luck seemed to have improved in general, starting with the impossibly lucky coincidence that Bette Buxom's destination had turned out to be St Charming's, of all places!

Dobbin had risen splendidly to the occasion and had got them there just in time to see Bette's coach turn in through the imposing gates and go rattling off up the drive.

"I don't get it," Ray had said, staring in puzzlement at the large sign above the school gates. "Look where we are! St Charmin's. But this is where them rotten princes took the guv! What's that Buxom woman doin' 'ere? D'you reckon she's come to return 'is rightful property or summin'?"

"*Return* property? Bette Buxom? Don't make me laugh," Ruby had said scornfully. "She's selling it, of course. Don't you remember anything? Like Doug saying about the Headmaster being a mad collector? It's obvious, isn't it? He's one of her regular clients. Anyway, it couldn't have worked out better for us. We'll be able to kill two birds with one stone. Right, you stay here with Dobbin."

"Why? Where are you going?"

"I'm going to follow her in, of course. It'll be a doddle to someone with my woodcraft skills. I shall sneak along behind her, pinch the rug when no one's looking, find Doug and rescue him. You can expect us back within the hour. Be prepared for a quick getaway."

Both Ray and the horse had sighed. Hanging around together preparing for a quick getaway was getting to be a way of life. And they didn't even like each other much.

Back in the corridor, Ruby jumped away from the door as there came the sudden, jarring sound of a hand bell, followed by the sound of a chair scraping back. Heart thumping, she scuttled back to her hiding place behind the Noble Founder. She was only just in time. There came the sound of hurrying footsteps and the hall porter came bustling back down the corridor. He knocked briskly on the Headmaster's door, and then went in, closing the door behind him.

A few moments later it opened again and Bette Buxom emerged. She had a satisfied smirk on her face, and her handbag looked a lot heavier than it had when she came in.

"A pleasure to do business with you as always, Headmaster," she was saying. "I wish all my customers 'ad such a discerning eye."

In her wake trundled a hairy old man in a squeaking Bath chair, which was being propelled forward by the hall porter. This must be the unpleasantly named Josiah T. Whiplash, Headmaster. Ruby flattened herself against the wall.

"The pleasure's all mine, dear lady. Although it must be said you do, ha ha, drive a hard bargain."

"Oooh, tee hee, I'm not just a pretty face, Headmaster, oh dear me no. No need to see me out, I know me way."

"Wouldn't dream of it, dearest lady, the very least I can do. Lock the door, Spittoon, lock the door. I've just made a most valuable purchase."

"A very wise precaution, Headmaster," nodded Bette as Henry Spittoon fussed with his bunch of keys. "There's some very unscrupperlus people about, I know that for a fact. You can't trust nobody."

"You are so right, dearest lady. Watch what

you're doing, Spittoon, you're nearly tipping me out …"

The Bath chair went bumping down the stairs, and the sound of their voices faded. As soon as the coast was clear, Ruby went into action.

Picking the lock was a matter of moments, involving some nifty work with a hairgrip, scissors and a small pot of candle grease.

(One of Ruby's more useful woodcraft skills included breaking and entering, vital because her sisters usually ganged up on her and locked her out of the bedroom.)

There was a click, and the lock snapped back. With a smug little smile of satisfaction, Ruby pushed open the door, slipped in and bolted it behind her.

Doug's rug lay forlornly on the polished floorboards. It looked every bit as depressingly tired and worn out here as it had on Bette's scarlet shagpile. Ruby noted new stains that appeared to be quite recent. Contributions from Bette's dogs, she suspected. Still, appearances could often be deceptive. And Gran wasn't often wrong about such things.

Ruby reached into her basket and pulled out a small piece of paper. On it, in Gran Grubb's spidery writing, was a list of words.

Feeling rather foolish, she walked to the middle of the rug. She set down her basket, straightened up, cleared her throat and read out the first one.

Which was, of course, the Hartustandi word for "up".

"Oma Phli Pinekk," intoned Ruby, trying to sound as magical and commanding as she could, but unsure of the pronunciation.

And the rug moved. It did, it really did. There was a little shiver beneath her feet, and a small cloud of dust rose. It felt almost as though the rug was drawing breath.

"Oma Phli Pinekk!" Ruby tried again, making every effort to roll the consonants as Gran Grubb had advised.

She was getting better. The rug gave quite a promising ripple this time, and the edges curled up in an eager sort of way. It was uncanny. But it still didn't leave the floor.

"Come on, come on, take off you stupid mat!" muttered Ruby through clenched teeth. And that was when she heard the ominous sound of steel-capped shoes hurrying back once again down the corridor. Oh no. Josiah T. Whiplash had forgotten his cane or a spare blanket something, and had sent the hall porter back for it!

The footsteps stopped outside the door, and Ruby heard the jangling of keys.

"Oh my flippin' 'eck," gulped Ruby ...

And the rug went up! It gave a surge, then a lurch, and up it went, about two metres, where it floated over the polished floorboards admiring its own reflection.

Taken by surprise, Ruby lost her balance and fell forward on to her knees. Her basket rolled towards the edge and she only just stopped it from tipping over. Her floundering hands gripped the edge of the hovering rug, which dipped a bit, drifted forward, bumped gently into a bookshelf, then steadied.

It was a very strange feeling, kneeling on a painfully scratchy rug which was hovering in midair. Ruby wouldn't like to admit it, but she wasn't good at heights. Heights made her queasy. But now wasn't the time to think of that.

Outside the door, Henry Spittoon stopped rattling his key around uselessly in the lock and stiffened.

"Hoi!" he barked. "What's goin' hon hin there?"

And he pushed at the door.

The bolt was a flimsy one. After the third lunge, it gave way, precipitating Henry Spittoon forward into the study — just in time to see, of all things, a girl in a red cloak fly out of the window on the Headmaster's brand-new ghastly antique carpet!

CHAPTER TWENTY-TWO
IT FLIPPIN' WELL FLIES!

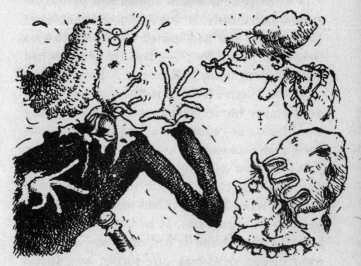

Dobbin breaks out — Doug's thoughts on ballroom dancing — Mr Plumfairy suffers from shock — Ruby flies by and Doug once again takes to his heels

Out by the school gates, Dobbin waited on its own. Ray had discovered an unexpected coin deep in some forgotten leather cranny or other, and had gone running off down the road in hot pursuit of a passing vendor of hot potatoes.

Ray and the potato-seller were now deep in meaningful conversation. There was a choice of three fillings — grey jelly, brown lumps or green splodge. It was Ray's sort of food. He was having trouble making up his mind.

Dobbin was restless. It shifted and pawed the ground impatiently. It was a very different horse to the horse that had started out from Morania three — or was it four? — days ago. Then, it had been a slow, solid, dull horse. A horse whose motto had been Never Trot If You Can Plod. A predictable horse. The sort of horse nobody would look at twice. An anonymous horse. A horse with no name.

It was now a changed animal. Instead of a coach-pulling sort of horse, it was now a getaway horse. It was a horse that had seen action. It had been to foreign parts. It had been chased by howling hill goblins. It had eaten edelweiss in a spontaneous, devil-may-care sort of way. It had got sick, and recovered. It had been shot at by a highwayman. It had chased after a coach. It had lived a little.

Best of all, it now had a name. That name was Dobbin. In the best of all possible worlds the horse would have preferred something like Flaming Arrow or maybe Flash The Wonder Horse — but Dobbin would do.

Dobbin chewed on its bit, remembering. It didn't dwell on its ignominious entry into Nubb tied behind a chicken wagon. Instead, it skipped to the bit by the water trough outside Ruby's granny's, where it had caused a bit of a scene, rolling its eyes and generally acting a mite temperamental. It had enjoyed that bit. It imagined itself telling that bit to the nags in the stable back home.

And talking of stables — there was a rather promising, though distant, smell in the air. It wafted from behind the gates. It told of warm straw and nice rubdowns and kindly pats from whistling grooms. It hinted at yummy nosebags and the occasional sugar lump. Best of all, it spoke of the flattering attention of other horses. Mares, perhaps. Mares who would flutter their eyelashes and listen admiringly to gallant tales of equestrian derring-do told by a dashing brown stranger.

Dobbin nuzzled at the gate, which swung open. It found itself staring down a long, tree-lined driveway leading to an imposing building with tall white columns and a sweeping flight of steps, before which Bette's hired coach waited.

The driveway had horse appeal. It was everything that a Moranian road wasn't. It was smooth, dry and pothole-free. Just the ticket for a frisky little canter. And that smell — that lovely smell ...

"Oi!" shouted Ray, coming back up the road with his splodge-filled hot potato. "Dobbin! Where d'you think you're off to? Come back 'ere this minute!"

It didn't, of course.

* * *

Back in the gym, Doug's ballroom-dancing class had come to another halt.

"What do you mean, you don't *feel* like dancing?" enquired Mr Plumfairy, red-faced with exasperation. He could see he was going to have real trouble with the new boy. Not only had the untidy young lout sulked through the entire paso doble, he was now refusing to take a partner for the old-time sequence.

"I've only got one shoe," Doug pointed out, waggling his blistered left foot which protruded through the shredded remains of his hose. He had recovered from the stitch, but without an improvement in the footwear department he doubted that he could run any more. It was unfortunate, but at the moment escape seemed out of the question.

"I can see that, boy, I can see that. Well, princes have had to attend balls with a lot worse things missing than that, I can tell you. When you're out there dancing with the princess of your dreams, you'll have to come up with a better excuse than that."

"All right, then, how about this — I hate ballroom dancing and I don't see what it's got to do with running a kingdom. How's that?"

There was a general gasp of shocked disapproval. This was rebellion on an unprecedented scale. You just didn't say that sort of thing at St Charming's. Not unless you wanted to jog ten times around the running track carrying a heavy glass coffin containing a full-sized waxwork of Snow White.

Or, even worse, go and see the Headmaster.

Mr Plumfairy was beside himself. Not only was the new boy late, untidy, rough and insolent with absolutely no sense of rhythmical timing, he was daring to criticise the subject that was dearest to Mr Plumfairy's heart. Why, everyone knew that important business deals (royal marriages in particular) were hammered out on the dance floor. A good working knowledge of the foxtrot was essential if you were to land your rich princess.

Mr Plumfairy turned red, then white, then weak at the knees. Two boys had to help him over to Mrs Plunket's piano stool. One fanned him with a sheet of music while Mrs Plunket administered smelling salts. The class gathered round, grateful for the interruption.

"Now you've done it," announced Frederick of Mushcatoon gleefully from the door of the changing room. He limped forward, a cold flannel pinned around his ankle. "Now you're for it. And I'm writing to my father about you. He's an emperor, you know ..."

But Doug wasn't listening. Something outside had attracted his attention. Frederick of Mushcatoon followed his gaze — and was surprised to see a brown horse trotting past with a determined air. Dragging along behind, on the end of a long rope, was a fat, red-faced, common-looking leather-clad guard-type in a balaclava. Eyes popping, the uncouth fellow dug his heels in and strained at the rope — then was unceremoniously yanked forward into a stumbling little run. His sweating red face peered anxiously into the gymnasium, obviously seeking help — and spotted Doug.

"Guv!" shouted Ray. "There you are! Come on out 'ere an' give us a 'and, will yer? I can't 'old it! It's makin' for the wassit! Stable!"

And he was dragged off around the corner.

Then something even more amazing happened. Something that made Frederick of Mushcatoon's jaw drop open and stay there for some considerable time.

Ruby sailed into view!

She sat cross-legged and bolt upright on the rug. One white-knuckled hand clutched at her basket, the other held a slip of paper. Her face was a waxen mask of terror and she appeared to be muttering something between clenched teeth.

Doug's rug looked a lot more imposing in the air than it had on the floor. The air was obviously its natural element. So impressive was its performance that you didn't even notice the dog-hairs or the stains. It floated along purposefully with only the barest suggestion of a wobble, maintaining a sedate speed and an unadventurous height of about two metres above the ground.

This, however, was two metres higher than Ruby cared to be. She looked like she was about to be sick at any moment.

Doug gave a whoop and whacked the boggle-eyed Frederick of Mushcatoon on the back.

"It flies! The rug! Of course, *that's* what's special about it! IT FLIPPIN' WELL FLIES!"

And before anyone could register what was happening, he slipped off his one remaining shoe and made for the door at what can only be described as a frenzied hobble.

CHAPTER TWENTY-THREE
A VERY NICE ENDING

Escape through the window — The pursuit —
Conversation with an Ungracious Groom —
A multiple pile-up — Up and Down —
Ray gets a double ducking — Freedom at last

Josiah T. Whiplash was saying his final farewells
to Bette Buxom at the foot of the main steps. She
was just about to climb into her waiting cab, when
she heard the sound of running footsteps and
Henry Spittoon burst from the building and came
leaping down the steps three at a time. His face
was purple and his eyes bulged alarmingly.

"Did you see?" he gasped. "Did you see the

cheeky 'ussy come flyin' hout the window? Which way'd she go? Round the back, was it? Don't you worry, 'Eadmaster, Hi'm on 'er trail, heverything's hunder control."

"Eh? What? What's he say? What're you talking about, Spittoon?"

"Your nice new carpet, 'Eadmaster!" came the cry. "Some bloomin girl's just flown horf honnit! Hout your study window! Keep yer heye hon the sky!"

And he ran off round the corner, legs pumping like pistons and steel toecaps striking blue sparks on the gravel. Behind him, Josiah T. Whiplash let out a howl of anger which wouldn't have disgraced a hungry wolf with a thorn in its paw, a bad headache and a nasty case of ear mites.

Also running like mad was Doug.

"RUBY!" he croaked after the retreating rug. "It's me, Doug! Wait for me!"

At the sound of his voice, Ruby cast a terrified glance back over her shoulder. The rug gave a sideways lurch and collided with a tree. With a little sob, Ruby reached out and seized an overhanging branch. The rug bumped restlessly against the tree trunk, obviously keen to move off but not feeling quite right about leaving its passenger behind and helplessly dangling.

"Come on then!" shrieked Ruby. "D'you think this is easy or something? We've got to get out of here right now. I'm being chased!"

"Who by?"

"The porter. The Headmaster. Bette Buxom. Everybody. Oh, do hurry up and get on, will you? I can't hold it steady much longer."

"How can I? You're two metres up in the air! Bring it down a bit."

"I can't! I can't! I can't do DOWN yet. I can only do UP. All the instructions are in Hartustandi. DOWN's written on this piece of paper, but I can't pronounce it."

"Then help me up! Let me have a go!"

"I can't! It'll wobble! I'll fall!"

Just then, there came a shout from behind. Bearing down upon them was a screaming mob of ballroom dancers, led by Mr Plumfairy (recovered), Mrs Plunket (waving a rolled sheet of music) and Frederick of Mushcatoon (also miraculously cured).

"I think this is where I wake up and discover it's all a dream," said Doug hopefully, to no one in particular. "Isn't it? Don't I?"

But it wasn't and he didn't.

Over in the stable yard, Henry Spittoon was holding an impatient conversation with an Ungracious Groom.

"Yes, yes, that's what Hi said, hidiot! Hay girl hon a flying carpet! Did she pass this way, yes hor no?"

"Lord love a duck, Mr Spittoon, so that's what

it were! You coulda knocked me dahn wiv a fevver, she flew past 'ere only a coupla minutes ago, cor blimey what a turn up eh, well I'll go to the foot of our stairs, I fort I were seein' fings, cor, strike a light–"

"Yes, yes, hall right, hall right, which way did she go?"

"Rahnd the corner, boss, bold as brass she were, flyin' carpet, eh? Cor, swipe me if that don't beat all …"

Henry Spittoon left him to it and ran on down the path. He rounded the corner with a screech of toecaps …

… And found himself on a collision course with a determined-looking brown horse who was hellbent for the stables. Henry's brain immediately instructed him to stop and take evasive action. But his legs had taken on a kind of life of their own, and refused to stop running.

But mowing down humans just wasn't Dobbin's style. It swerved politely to the left to let Henry Spittoon pass. A short way behind, red in the face and a bit battered but still clinging grimly on to the tautly-stretched rope, stumbled Ray. Henry Spittoon ran slap into the rope, which acted like an elastic band and sent him staggering backwards into the lap of Josiah T. Whiplash, who at that moment came bowling around the corner in his Bath chair, waving his cane wildly in the air and bellowing "Stop, thief! Get 'er, Spittoon!

Stick the cheeky gel in Detention!"

Behind Josiah came Bette Buxom, teetering along on unsuitably high heels, unable to resist the chance of seeing a real flying carpet in action. Whoever would have believed it! If only she'd known, she would have charged a hundred times as much! She could have kicked herself.

She collided painfully with the Bath chair, which slowly keeled over. Josiah T. Whiplash, Henry Spittoon and Bette sprawled on the ground in a furious tangle of arms, legs, plaid rugs, and red petticoats. One of the chair's wheels came loose and rolled back down the driveway, neatly tripping up Matron who, scenting an accident, was hurrying gleefully to the scene armed with a portable stretcher and a large bottle of iodine.

In the meantime, Dobbin had finally made it to the stable yard where it was currently chomping away at a big bale of hay in a corner. Ray, of course, had predictably landed in the water trough. To his credit, he still had hold of the rope.

By now, teachers and pupils were pouring out of the classrooms to see what all the fuss was about. Rumours were spreading like wildfire. There was a madman loose in the grounds. A wild horse was running amok. Mr Whippy had finally gone bonkers and was running some sort of race with Henry Spittoon and Bette Buxom from The Laughing Footpad ...

Someone somewhere had seen a girl on a flying carpet!

Of all the daft things, that was the one that got them.

"Ha, ha ha!" laughed all the princes. "A girl on a flying carpet? Pull the other leg, it's got hose on."

Meanwhile, back at the carpet ...

"Ruby! Reach down and give me a hand up!" commanded Doug. It was a desperate situation. They hadn't moved an inch and the dancing mob was almost upon them.

"I can't, I tell you. I'll fall!"

"Hah! Call yourself a woodcutter's daughter," jeered Doug. "Whatever happened to all that resourcefulness you're always going on about?"

That did the trick. He knew it would. In seconds, he was grabbed by his ruff and one arm and hauled roughly up on to the rug, which bobbled about alarmingly.

"Oh my flippin' 'eck ..." gulped Doug.

That did it. Mr Plumfairy, Mrs Plunket and the ravening ballroom dancers stopped short, their mouths dropping open, as Doug and Ruby soared skyward with an audible whoosh.

"Idiot!" screamed Ruby. "Now see what you've done!"

"Eh? Me? What did I do?"

"You said the words. There, look, see? OMA

PLHI PINEK. That means 'up' in Hartustandi. Quick, look up 'down' before we go into orbit!"

Trying hard not to look past the edges of the rug, where the earth was rapidly dropping away, Doug peered at the crumpled piece of paper.

"What's this? Is this an 'o'? Or a 'd'? It looks like IDREE something. IDREE ... LEE LI K'TUGOL OWR. Something like that."

"Well, that can't be right, can it? We're still rising. Oh, please, please do something. I'd *really* like to go lower. I think I'm going to be sick."

And down they plunged.

"What did you just say?" bellowed Doug, over the sound of the wind whistling about his ears and Ruby's screams. He was finding it hard to speak with his stomach in his mouth.

"Ahhhhhh! I said I think I'm going to be sick."

"No, before that."

"I said I'd really like to go lower."

"That's it! Don't you see? IDREE LEE LI K'TUGOL OWR. You said it right. Hey, it's easy when you know how!"

"So what's it say for STOP before we crash into the stable yard? Come on, I thought you said it was easy!"

"All right, all right, I'm doing my best. Your gran's got terrible writing. Let me see, we need to straighten out a bit, don't we ... er ... ah, this should do it. FULSTEE MAR HED."

* * *

Down below, Ray sat wearily on the edge of the water trough. Dobbin's hindquarters were now sticking out of the stable door. It had finished the hay bale and was enquiring about pudding. From inside came the sound of wild whinnying as the school horses neighed up the situation.

Ray was just about to remove a sodden boot in order to pour out the water when something above him caught his eye, and he looked up. At first glance he thought it was a giant bat bearing down on him — but he didn't stop to check. He threw himself backwards just in time, and the large flying thing passed right through the space where his head had been a split second before. For the second time in the last five minutes he hauled himself out of the water trough and knuckled green algae out of his eyes.

The thing that had buzzed him circled three times over the stable roofs then shot off in the direction of the playing fields.

"What is it?" screamed a freckle-faced stable lad, dropping his buckets and running for cover. "Lore love us, squire, whatever can it be?"

"Don't you know what that is?" said Ray with great pride. "Wassa matter wiv yer eyesight, pal? Thassa flyin' wassit, that is. Only one left in the world. An' it belongs to My Guv."

He raised his voice and bellowed importantly skywards.

"Wait fer me, Guv!" he bellowed. "Don't you

worry! Hang on tight, now, make a space, I'm comin'!"

With great determination, he hauled on the rope. The horse backed away from the stable. Ray came squelching up and grabbed at its mane.

"Stand still, you!" he ordered, attempting without success to haul himself on to Dobbin's broad back. "Well, give us a leg up, then," he snapped at the freckle-faced stable lad, who obediently linked his hands.

"Right, you blinkin' animal, it's time you earned your keep. Now then — follow that rug!"

Dobbin was only too happy to oblige. It was an excellent chance to prove itself to the stable horses, who were a disappointing lot as well as being mean with their sugar lumps. It shot off at a full gallop towards the main gate, Ray clinging grimly to its back.

Far above, Doug began to laugh. "What's so funny?" asked Ruby.

"Look below and you'll see."

Ruby looked and giggled.

"Poor Ray. I almost think I'm starting to feel sorry for him. What d'you think. Shall we go down for him?"

"Soon," said Doug. "Not yet. I don't think there's room for Dobbin. Golly, we're causing quite a stir."

They were indeed. Far below, the grounds of St Charming's were dotted with dozens of tiny figures all milling about, shouting and gesticulating skywards. More and more were coming to join them.

"I really don't think I'd have fitted in at St Charming's, you know," remarked Doug. "I said so all along."

"I think I'm getting over my height sickness!" shouted Ruby above the wind. "It's quite fun when you get used to it, isn't it? Where shall we go first? Back to Gran's for a fish tea? Or perhaps we should make enquiries about where to sell the carpet? Gran says it's worth a king's ransom. Imagine your dad's face when you go back with the money! What d'you think they'll do with it?"

"Dad'll want to gamble it away. Mum'll want to get her hair done and have the palace redecorated. But I shan't let them. I shall make them invest it all in a decent drainage system, so that Moranian beetroots will be great once more. But first I'm going to take a holiday. I reckon I deserve it after all I've been through. I'll throw out the Costume and buy myself some new clothes. Then you can show me around Nubb. Show me some of the ten thousand surprises. It's funny. I didn't think I liked surprises. Life has been very surprising recently — but on the whole, I've almost sort of quite enjoyed it."

"Me too," said Ruby. "And I think a holiday would make a very nice ending."

"Tell you what!" Doug bawled back happily.

"Don't let's go anywhere special right now. Let's just fly around for a while!"

"Good idea. Come on — let's go up a bit!"

"Oh my flippin' 'eck!" they both screamed …

And up they went.

WHAT HAPPENED

For the tidy-minded who don't like loose ends lying around all over the place, here's what happened.

Jacques Cravat never did find out that he had been doubled-crossed by Bette. However, one night down at The Laughing Footpad he was spotted by a talent scout and went into show business, where he earned a reasonable living doing cabaret and summer pantomime and signing autographs for adoring maidens (only the stupid ones).

Gran Grubb passed her exams, became a practising Witch and gave up her day job. She offered the fish stall to Ray, but, as he explained, he already had a full time job guarding the Guv.

Josiah T. Whiplash and Bette Buxom had words. Josiah wanted his money back and Bette wanted to keep it. They agreed in the end to split it — but their beautiful friendship got a little flaky round the edges. Josiah grieved for his stolen rug for a day or two by taking it out on his staff, his pupils and, of course, Henry Spittoon. Then he spotted a spectacularly ugly twelfth-century soup tureen that he simply had to have and forgot all about it.

When Bette got back, there had been another Troll raid and The Laughing Footpad had been stripped of everything except the tables (which were nailed to the floor). Terry had packed his saddlebags and left for pastures new and one of the dogs had finished up the sausage rolls and been sick all over the sofa. It had been one of those days.

As for what happened to Doug, Ruby, Ray and Dobbin ...

No. That's another story. You'll have to wait for that one.